# A TRICK OF THE DARK

# A
# TRICK OF THE DARK

## Kenneth Lillington

*faber and faber*

LONDON · BOSTON

*For Susan*

First published in Great Britain in 1994
by Faber and Faber Limited
3 Queen Square London WC1N 3AU

Photoset in Palatino by Keyboard Services, Luton
Printed in England by Clays Ltd, St Ives Plc.

A CIP record for this book is available from the
British Library

ISBN 0 571 17068 4

2 4 6 8 10 9 7 5 3 1

# CHAPTER ONE

WHEN SHE WAS eight years old, Kate Crimonesi had a quarrel with her father. It was one-sided, because he didn't quarrel back, but she never forgot it, and by the time she was eighteen she had recalled it countless times.

She had been glancing at a full-page photograph in a Sunday colour supplement. It showed the corner of 'a woodland garden' with an old gentleman standing in it. There was an article about him on the opposite page. His name was R. J. Bodkin and he was a professor of mediaeval literature. This in itself was hardly enough to make him a household name, but he had recently acquired wild fame, because he had written a book which everyone in the world was reading and had become the centre of a cult. It was a fantasy novel entitled *The Gnomes of Yggsdragarth*. No one was more surprised at its success than the professor, because he had written it solely to please himself, although it must have cost him a deal of labour, for it ran to eleven hundred pages.

None of this much interested Kate, aged eight, and the picture itself would only have held her fleeting attention, had not something suddenly caught her eye. She exclaimed, 'There's an elf in this picture!'

'Go on?' said her father absently, and went on writing his notes.

But Kate was open-mouthed. The picture showed a grassy

patch with stepping-stones, leading to a broad mound of bushes. Next to the baggy-trousered professor, and to his left, appeared the face of the elf, a farthing of a face, cute and mischievous, with pointed ears, a pointed cap and black pinpoints for eyes. Once seen, you couldn't ignore it, and it was astonishing that Kate had not seen it before.

'You seem interested, Katie,' said her father with mild curiosity. 'What is this picture?'

'It says the garden of Professor Bodkin.'

'Oh, that!' He frowned. 'I don't recall seeing anything of the kind when I looked at it. Show me.'

'There you are.'

'Katie,' said Mr Crimonesi reproachfully, 'you know quite well there's no elf in this picture.' And then, to turn it to a joke, 'You start seeing things, they'll put you in a home, you know.'

'I'm not.'

'Hang on. You mean these leaves make a kind of face, something like that? I can't see it myself, yet –'

'You can, you can!' Kate was exasperated. 'It's *there*, look, it's *there*!' And indeed the elf's impudent face dominated the picture. How could he possibly miss it? 'It's there, there, *there*!' She jabbed the picture with her finger. 'How can you be so silly?'

Her mother looked up and said 'Hey!' Her father said, 'If it were there you wouldn't need to lose your temper, would you, because I'd see it too.'

He never lost his temper and never raised his voice. Kate was moved to tears of frustration. As a final insult he told her that she was tired. That was too much; she flung away sobbing and pounded off to bed, stamping with all her might on every stair.

'You should have said you saw it for the sake of peace and quiet,' said Kate's mother.

'Oh, but see for yourself.'

2

'Yes, I have seen it.' Mrs Crimonesi took the magazine nevertheless and glanced at the picture. 'You're quite right, of course. I don't know what got into her. No, let her calm down. I'll go up to her in a minute.'

When she did go up Kate was a sack-shaped lump under the bedclothes, and after calling her quietly once or twice Mrs Crimonesi retreated.

Mr Crimonesi was sorry to have upset Kate, but it was against his nature to pretend. He was a lecturer in mathematics, much admired in his profession. As far as it is possible for human flesh and blood to be, he was a pure mathematician. His ideal world would have been one created out of sheer intelligence. He had long discarded the Catholic religion of his childhood; or perhaps he had buried it. He had been known to declare that if God existed, He would have to be awarded a first-class degree in mathematics. He did not say who would award it. He disapproved of nearly all works of fiction, and had no time at all for legend or fantasy. He turned a sardonic eye on Imagination itself, which he believed, not without reason, was responsible for most of the evil in the world.

'She's asleep,' said his wife, returning.

She was not. Kate lay under the bedclothes fierce and shuddering. She had her father's logical mind and to be contradicted in the face of objective fact really distressed her, it wounded her like injustice. But her shuddering subsided, her anger cooled, she was ashamed that she had lost her temper, and when, with her eyes closed, she saw the elfin face on her eyelids, she thought that it was mocking her for doing so. But it merged into its leafy background and was lost in a green blur, and by the time her father looked in at her she was fast asleep.

He made a small compassionate grimace and left her room, composing in his head some tactful overtures he would make to her in the morning, and went downstairs to lock up for the night. He picked up the colour supplement and took it over to the pile of papers being accumulated for recycling, and glanced once more at the picture of Professor Bodkin, that traitor to adult thought. *The Gnomes of Yggsdragarth*! It wasn't even pronounceable. And then he saw the elf. It was there, the tiny impudent face, just above a hosta and on a level with Professor Bodkin's right ear. He had scarcely time to gasp when it was gone again. There must be, he reasoned, some chemical in the paper that caused this deception. He turned the picture this way and that, squinting at it, and even shook it, as if the face were somehow loose inside it, but nothing he could do would bring it back.

Well, Kate had evidently been in the right. He put the magazine in a drawer and resolved to discuss the picture again the next day, but as a matter of fact he never did. Kate happened to be on half-term from school and was still in bed when he left in the morning. Other obstacles presented themselves, but the truth was that he was reluctant to reopen the subject at all, for fear that Kate would still see something that he could not. As for Kate, she never bore grudges. Life was too demanding and exciting for her to dwell on any one matter for long, and she didn't mention elves again. She did, however, read *The Gnomes of Yggsdragarth* in guilty secrecy, and enjoyed it immensely like everyone else. In this she was aided and abetted by a certain Aunt Julia, who had once been her father's teacher; but this is to anticipate. The years went by, the picture stayed in the drawer, and the Crimonesis continued to live in intellectual harmony.

At eighteen, Kate had passed her A Level exams and had buried any inclination to fantasy under numerous layers of reason and logic. At this stage she was probably more sure of herself and the world than she would ever be again. She had inherited her father's brain and found mental effort easy. She had also inherited valuable qualities from her mother, who was English. She knew that on this island it is bad form to be clever and was fortunate enough to have dark Italian good looks that distracted people from any such suspicion. She got a holiday job working in a china shop and awaited her entry to university.

Kate never forgot the incident of ten years before, but it was the quarrel she remembered, rather than the elf. It had been nothing – a storm in a teacup, but it stood out above all other tiffs and fallings out as if it had some peculiar significance. She informed herself that there was doubtless a scientific reason for this. Then one night she saw the elf again.

Or rather, its reflection.

She had changed into a dressing gown, switched on her table lamp, and sat down without drawing her curtains. She often did this, out of a curious vanity. The house was old and her bedroom had a bay window with five panes, angled round, so that she could see five reflections of herself, and in the subdued light at the window these were softened and flattering. She shook loose her black hair. The five reflections did the same, as reflections should. But in the central pane alone the figure of the elf loomed up and sat down beside her.

Her immediate reaction, excusably enough, was that this was the reflection of something *in the room*. She gave a screech and jumped up on to her bed holding up the skirts of her dressing gown like any silly Victorian girl. A live rat in her room would be bad enough, but this was far worse than a rat. She pulled the light cord over her bed, flooded the room with light, and stared round at every square yard of it. But there was nothing in the room. She sat, cross-legged and tousled, on her bed and stared in dismay at what must be a disconnected shadow. And then – so

5

blinding is panic that she had forgotten this – she recognized that there were not five reflections of the elf, as there were of her, but only one, and while all her own reflections had been jumping and twisting about, this one had stayed perfectly still.

Gingerly she resumed her seat at her table and looked at him. He was rather faint in the full light, but he was there all right, and if she drew her curtains he would still be there, not like a mirror reflection, more like a ghost. She got up again, looking over her shoulder at him with every step, and switched off the ceiling light. The image sharpened up in the shadow. He was the very picture of the conventional elf, all in green, with a pointed cap, a tunic scalloped at the hem, tights and boots whose rims curled over like petals. His face was a perfect oval, with dark liquid eyes, comparatively enormous. He was very pretty, and would have been charming on a postcard.

Kate said 'Hallo' in a feeble voice. How did one speak to an elf? She supposed vaguely that one started with 'O!' and addressed him as 'Thou'. He sat beside her reflection as still as a Buddha, until with a sudden jerk he turned his head and looked up at her, so that she saw him in profile. She got another shock. He was old.

And in this position, not pretty at all. The angle of his jaw was like that of a pike. Kate felt as one might on seeing a skeleton or an X-ray: this was his real self stripped of beauty. But he turned his head and became pretty again, and then in a blink he was gone altogether, leaving her five reflections looking distractedly about.

Steeling herself, Kate opened the window and looked out into the dark in the weak hope of finding a natural cause for the illusion, but saw nothing but the back garden illuminated by the moon. She sat down and thought everything over. She had always been proud of her lucid mind, but perhaps there was a unique flaw in it that made her see elves? Was she slightly mad? She recalled with distress that incident of ten years ago. Had she been equally deluded then? How humiliating to have been wrong all this time. On the other hand, could deluded people question their delusions?

The other explanation was that the elf really had turned up, not in person, but in the form of his own ghost, so to speak. Not that that consoled her. A conventional ghost would have been more acceptable – a weeping maiden or a spectre in chains – people were sympathetic to ghost stories and would cap them with ones of their own. But elves! they were for kids; they peeped coyly round mushrooms. Unless you happened to look at one sideways, in which case it looked older than all the reptiles, and just as cold-blooded.

She wished that she could consult Aunt Julia on the matter, for she was an ally with whom Kate had shared many secrets, but one would have to go about that very carefully. It might get to her father. He would be alarmed, and would talk about psychotherapy.

She drew her curtains, very thoroughly, switched off the table lamp and got into bed. She lay with her eyes closed, but the image of the elf remained, sometimes full-face and sweet and sometimes in profile and angular like a pike. Her mind had quietened now and was back on its old track of scientific curiosity. 'Is this what it's like to be haunted?' she wondered.

# CHAPTER TWO

KATE HAD A BOYFRIEND, one year older than herself, who was studying for a degree in music. His name was Adam Longfellow and he played the flute exceedingly well. There were disadvantages in having a musician as a mate; one could look forward to lonely evenings, and players of wind instruments, sadly, had to avoid kissing, as it made the lips inappropriately soft. But there, he was talented. He had the gift of perfect pitch, so that if you scraped your chair on the floor he would remark of the squeak, 'That's C sharp.' He could also remember any tune on hearing it once and play it without fault. He took his gift cheerfully for granted and would play anything, classical or pop, with equal readiness. (Snobbery in art, like the artistic temperament, is for amateurs.) This was just as well, because in this summer vacation he was playing with a local quintet, and they had engagements of all kinds.

He was tall, angular and sandy haired, and he had a lopsided grin which Kate found attractive, although as a rule she preferred symmetry. Early in their acquaintance she had made him sit still while she critically examined his face.

'One half is a different shape from the other.'

'Yes? I don't look at it much.'

'Your face is like a pair of odd socks. You've pulled it out of shape fluting.'

'Yes, I expect I'll end up biting one of my ears.'

9

'Can't wind you up, can I?'

Adam had her father's approval too, fortunately. As is not uncommon with mathematicians, Professor Crimonesi liked music, and thought a musical score very satisfying to look at. He may even have preferred reading it to hearing it. Anyway, he liked Adam, who was lucky not to have been born a poet.

Kate said, as they sat in the café, 'Have I ever told you a thing that happened to me when I was eight? I was looking at this magazine –'

'– and saw an elf. Yes, you have. About ten times.'

'Oh. Well, just listen to this.' Kate went on to explain recent events.

If Adam had doubts he did not express them.

'When was this, Katie?'

'Three nights ago.'

'And you haven't seen it since?'

'No, because now I draw my curtains before I put the light on, but I know he's there behind them. I know this all sounds like some hang-up from childhood and I've wondered a lot about that, but I do believe that I saw what I saw as a matter of objective fact. But why should he pop up again after ten years? And another thing: that *Observer* colour supplement must have been seen by, oh I don't know, thousands of people, hundreds of thousands. Why me then? Why shouldn't thousands of them have seen it as well as me?'

'Perhaps they did.'

'What, and said nothing about it?'

'I see what you mean. Have you told your dad about this?'

'Good God, no.'

'No, silly question.'

'All the same,' said Kate, wrinkling her brow, 'I've got a feeling he's on to me. He wears a kind of puzzled expression, and that's so unlike him, nothing puzzles him. I've tried bouncing around all jaunty like and calling him 'Pa-pa', you know, heavy Italian accent, it's an old joke between us, but he doesn't really fall for it. I'm sure he's on to me. We're pretty close, you know.' Adam nodded ruefully. 'Well, I don't like him worried, he doesn't deserve it. I mean, I don't want to resurrect an old argument. I mean –'

'Yes, sure,' said Adam. 'Has your mother noticed anything?'

'I don't think so.'

'Professor Bodkin's garden,' mused Adam.

'Hm? Yes, that is what the picture was of.'

'Do you know where it is? I do, anyway. It's very near here, about three miles away. He lives in a place called Dovecot Lane.'

'What about it? You're not suggesting I should call on him?'

'Yes, actually. Only I meant us. I'd go with you.'

'Oh, Adam!'

'Well, you need protection. Elves are sexy little things, aren't they? Don't they carry off little girls? Anyway, if anyone can tell you anything about elves this professor can. The blurb on his books says he's soaked in folklore and I don't doubt he takes elves seriously. Quite a few great minds have. W. B. Yeats did. I reckon the professor would like to meet you. There have been a lot of in-depth critical studies of *The Gnomes of Yggsdragarth* and I expect they've driven him up the wall. And then you turn up, keeper of a personal elf. He'll go mad.'

'I wouldn't know how to begin.'

'We'll work something out.'

'My dad must never hear of it. He likes to think I'm a working model of pure reason. He'd worry himself sick.'

'I tell you what, we won't tell him, eh?'

'Adam, I love you.'

'It's the least you can do.'

'You look tired, Guido,' said Mrs Crimonesi.

'Mild eye strain,' said her husband. His large dark eyes did look heavier-lidded than usual. 'Too much squinting at hieroglyphics.'

'Remind me to buy some eye drops.' She gave him a curious glance, however. There had been something evasive about that mild semi-joke; normally he took his health very seriously. Something on his mind? But she said nothing.

Yes, something was on his mind. A green-clad elf with an impish smirk was on it. To begin with, he had been furious with his mind for entertaining anything so childish, but he was beginning to be alarmed.

He had first seen it in dreams. He would be giving a lecture and it would perch on his desk, cross-legged, left hand holding its right elbow, its chin cupped in its right hand. Its cuteness irritated him intensely. He dreaded, in these dreams, that his students would see it too and despise him for bringing it in, but he always woke up before this stage was reached, to his great relief. This dream occurred for four nights in succession, and then he saw it *after he woke up*, perched cross-legged on the ottoman under the window, grinning that grin. He saw it fade, as if his eyes were returning to normal after being dazzled, but his anxiety did not fade.

Of course, the figments of dreams did sometimes remain, momentarily, after the dreamer thought himself awake, but why should he dream this one dream so persistently? Perhaps this was a kind of guilt reaction for never having confessed to Kate what he had glimpsed in that picture? A psychological delayed reaction? He believed in psychology: it conveniently explained away so many spiritual problems; but he would never have considered seeking a psychologist's aid himself.

He was leading a summer vacation course in astronomy at the university. Astronomy was his hobby and he was saturated with its lore. His enthusiasm shone through his matter-of-fact delivery and his students were rapt. They found a statement like, 'There are some stars big enough to contain millions of our sun', full of romantic overtones. At forty-six he was a handsome man of good physique; he still had the slight, charming trace of a foreign accent and his polite, formal manner was almost provocative. He was not unaware of his appeal, but by behaving impeccably he both offset it and enhanced it. His wife was aware of it too, and was poised between pride and anxiety.

He was expounding the properties of red dwarfs when a green one appeared on an empty chair at the end of the front row and sat there nonchalant and cross-legged, with one arm draped over the handbag belonging to the woman on the chair next to it. He stopped speaking and stared at it so fixedly that the woman coloured slightly and transferred the bag to her lap as if afraid that it gave offence. In doing so she lifted it right *through* the creature as if through a sunbeam, and then, quite oblivious of her elfin neighbour, she directed at the Professor a look of pious attention. By now the whole group was uneasy. The Professor had given this lecture before and continued on automatic pilot but it was as if he were miming to a cassette, the personal dynamism was missing, and his students left the lecture room obscurely disturbed.

The elf had vanished, but Professor Crimonesi sat in the empty room for some minutes, glancing now and then quite pathetically at the empty chair, dreading that it might come back. He had no doubt that he had had a hallucination, but there was no comfort in that, because his mind must be out of control, and moreover this was becoming noticeable. The atmosphere at the lecture had been distinctly strained. And now he reflected, with dismay, that Kate herself had been treating him oddly of late – too jocular altogether, too much of the 'Pa-pa' nonsense, which was all very well as an occasional piece of banter but was soon overworked. She smiled at him too much, too, as if flirting with him. Their normal relationship was friendly but agreeably impersonal. She shared his interests, she loved discussion, but she had no taste for demonstrations of daughterly affection, and neither had he. A heart-to-heart talk was out of the question; it would have embarrassed them both. But he knew that she loved him deeply, and this recent behaviour of hers was a sure indication that she sensed his unease. She was on the brink of a new, demanding life and he didn't want her to enter it worried.

At this point he might even have overcome his reluctance to consult a psychologist, had his hallucination taken another form, but unwittingly like Kate herself, he found an elf humiliating. It was ludicrous, it could make him a laughing stock. Nevertheless, he admitted ruefully, he needed help.

His thoughts turned to Professor Bodkin, now long retired from teaching, and living on what Professor Crimonesi considered illgotten royalties. If, thrusting his tongue hard into his cheek, he consulted the old charlatan – in very general terms, of course, as one academic to another – he might learn enough of mythological mumbo-jumbo to combat his mental state. He would be shamelessly hypocritical, pretending to serious concern while storing up ammunition for mockery. Nothing could be more destructive to an obsession, he believed, than being able to laugh at it; and this he would do. 'Get right back up the airy mountain,' he imagined himself saying to the phantom elf. Yes: fight fire with fire.

He had never met Professor Bodkin, who had lectured in

another university, but he knew that he lived within easy reach in a place called Dovecot Lane. He rang Directory Enquiries, but was told that his number was ex-directory – not surprisingly, for the old boy must have been pestered in his heyday. A reply to a letter might take many days. Suddenly the matter became urgent, like calling the fire brigade. He would chance his luck and call personally. Now.

He rang his wife and told her that he might be home late. Her responses were delayed and rather cold. He shrugged regretfully and drove to Dovecot Lane.

It proved to be a side-turning off a road in an expensive estate where immense gardens kept the houses well apart. One costly dwelling stood, well back, at the entrance of the turning but once that was passed the road twisted away apparently into the green heart of nowhere, a cul-de-sac with Professor Bodkin's cottage at its very end.

Trees and bushes lined the left-hand side, while on the right there was a strip of grass and past that, the water of a small lake – only there was a wooded island in the lake which reduced it almost to a moat. A little rustic bridge crossed the water, and as the Professor reached this, driving very slowly, for the lane was now single track and full of bends, rain began to fall. But he saw, as he switched on his windscreen wipers, that while it was raining quite hard in the lane, on the other side of the bridge it was not.

He had heard of this phenomenon before – rain on one side of a railway carriage and sunshine on the other, for instance – but he had never witnessed it till now. Something, perhaps the excuse to delay his visit, impelled him to investigate it. He parked with his offside wheels on the strip of grass and crossed the bridge. The weather was chilly for late July, but here it was pleasantly mild. It was peaceful, so peaceful that it affected his senses almost like a drug. His eyes dwelt agreeably on all the shades of green, from silvery in the palest leaves to near black in the moss under his feet. But one would need a billhook to penetrate far into this wood. It was a mass of brambles, tangled up with wild strawberries. Convolvulus, with its white flowers, clung round everything. Overhead was an entanglement of branches, and Professor Crimonesi peered up, wondering if, after all, these simply formed an umbrella against the rain. This seemed to be borne out by a pitter-patter he had not heard before, but when he drew his attention to it he realized that it was not overhead, it came from the ground about his feet. And now he saw that the undergrowth everywhere was gently agitated. There was a scrabbling noise from a bush to his right. He saw a whiskered face and beady eyes. It was a rat.

It must have been one of thousands; the undergrowth was surely heaving with them. He stood still, and the twitching nose disappeared, reappeared, pointed itself up-ward, and withdrew again. Then, apparently reassured, the creature came into the open. Only the head was of a rat. The tiny body was human, and wore clothes.

The scrabbling noises multiplied, as if the denizens of the wood were massing for attack. The Professor had the feeling of being watched by thousands of eyes. He was only a few paces into the wood. He recrossed the bridge backwards to find that the shower had subsided to a drizzle. He got into his car and sat there for a while, leaning his head against the steering wheel.

Something was in the air in there, he reasoned, some aromatic plant that affected the senses. No, his senses had already been affected before he had come to this place. He was prey to some complex arising out of fatigue and guilt. Wasn't that merely jargon for 'I don't know what's wrong with me?' His muddled state of mind exasperated him. By a quirk of memory he was reminded of how Julia, Miss Mandible to him then, had read him fairy stories when he was a very small boy. 'Is it true?' he would demand. 'It is and it isn't,' she would reply. 'It's made up, of course, but in a way it's true.' But he'd have none of that. 'It's not true!' he would conclude, scowling. 'It's impossible!' He had wanted life in black and white. He still did.

It occurred to him that the wood must be at the back of Professor Bodkin's garden, separated only by a strip of water. To his extreme annoyance, the fancy came to his mind that the old man had enchanted it like some present-day Merlin. Shaking his head clear of such nonsense, he drove on, and came in sight of the Professor's timbered cottage.

The garden in which it stood was not large but beautifully planned and tended, in complete contrast to the tangled wood that lay behind it. It was surrounded by square-cut boxwood hedges, and within, leading up to the cottage, there was a parterre, a geometrical arrangement of brick path and more clipped box. A sundial broke the view between gate and cottage. Beyond this, to the right of the cottage from where he stood, were three broad terraces covered with rosemary and lavender, daisies, bronze fennel and thyme, and he could just make out the enclosure, farther back, where the photograph had been taken. Great care and intelligence had gone into the making of all this. No dull patches of lawn. And he liked the orderliness.

As he hesitated at the gate a gardener came in sight, trundling a wheelbarrow full of weeds, with a hoe lying across it. He lowered the barrow and came over, possibly even with menace; one pictured a hostile dog at his heels. He said 'Yes?' as if expecting Guido to open a case of samples and try to sell him something.

'Good afternoon. I am Professor Crimonesi. I was hoping that I might speak to Professor Bodkin.'

'Professor,' repeated the gardener with a kindling of respect. He was tall and thin and stooped a little, and with his iron-grey hair and side whiskers and his grave, lined face, he might have been an elder statesman or a warden of a very high church.

'Yes,' said Guido. 'I'm afraid I haven't an appointment but–'

A woman came from behind one of the boxwood bushes, her head high, as if she were permitting the drizzle to fall on her. 'I heard the word *professor*,' she said in a cultured voice. 'Are you a colleague?'

'In the broader sense of the word, yes. Professor Bodkin does not know me, but I have had some experiences that I think might interest him. Professor Crimonesi. I want his advice.'

'Professor Crimonesi. Margot Croupe. I am Professor Bodkin's secretary. This is Mr Hermitage. Have you not heard about Professor Bodkin? He had a severe stroke some while ago. He is quite incapable.'

'Oh dear.'

'Yes, it is very sad. What "experiences", Professor?'

He felt that he was in the witness box, and rather resented it. 'Forgive me,' he said, 'if I can't speak to Professor Bodkin I'd rather keep those to myself.'

They were polite, but a battle of wills had begun. The gardener, Hermitage, watched them guardedly. Margot Croupe said, 'One can speak to Professor Bodkin, Professor, but he cannot answer – and I must warn you that he finds some questions hurtful. Some interviewers upset him even before his illness. He was always a very private man. His great fame was most unwelcome to him and he was never happy to talk about himself. However–'

However, thought Guido, she's agog to hear my 'experiences', and so is the gardener. And indeed she continued, 'However, a visit from a member of his profession might please him. You may see him, Professor Crimonesi, but you must allow me to intervene if I see fit.'

Guido was not pleased that a man of his status should be given the permission of a secretary, and if Professor Bodkin was speechless an interview would have no point, but he felt committed to one now, and he let himself be led through the parterre and into the house. The gardener drifted after them as if his duties took him this way, but he left his barrow behind.

The cottage was old, seventeenth-century perhaps, and was furnished with pieces from various periods. A Georgian oak dresser base stood in the small hall, while the furniture in the sitting room included a chunky oak kneehole desk, an oak display cabinet full of china, and a mobile bath-chair in which reclined Professor Bodkin himself, motion-less as a waxwork and with less expression. Strangely, for the home of a lifelong scholar, there were no bookcases and not a sign of books.

Margot Croupe said, 'A visitor for you, Professor. This is Professor Crimonesi. He has some interesting things to tell you.'

She motioned to Guido to sit in a walnut wing armchair, and seated herself in its twin, from where she could oversee both of them. She had a stern, cream-coloured face and black hair, not glossy like Kate's but dry and dead, and piled up and fastened with a comb behind. Her eyes were also black and as dull as cloth buttons. They seemed to have the knack, without noticeably moving, of being every-where at once.

The gardener appeared outside the end windows. He appeared to be absorbed in a study of the wisteria on the wall beside them. A small window just above his head was open.

Professor Bodkin was a tiny, crumpled figure, strapped into the bathchair by a wide leather band round his middle, and banked round with cushions. His legs were covered with a blanket from which his slippered feet protruded.

His face was grey and sagging, and the pouches under his eyes were like a bloodhound's. His lips were loose and lightly covered with a white scum. His eyes were almost colourless. The right one showed signs of a cataract and stared glassily. The other, however, had a white rim round its pupil, but the *arc senilis* was phosphorescently bright, with the cold stare of an aged eagle. Guido felt his own robustness in facing him, and the man he had held in intellectual disdain for so long became pitiful, and yet that one eye threatened him. He said humbly, 'I have had – I am having – strange experiences, sir.'

He began telling his tale, beginning with Kate and the picture ten years before, and concluding with his dreams and the elfin apparition in the lecture room. He did not mention the rat-headed creature in the wood. The Professor's sound eye watched him without blinking. Guido, said, 'If I ask you a few questions, sir, can you nod or shake your head to them?' But Margot Croupe intervened.

'I'm sorry, I must stop you there, Professor. I cannot allow questions.'

'The wood,' said Guido with inner chagrin, 'I went into the wood –'

'You must see that the answers would require much more than nods or shakes of the head, and being unable to give them could be very distressing to him.'

It can't be very nice, either, thought Guido, to be talked about to his face like this, but with his usual courtesy he rose, bowed to the Professor, and withdrew. But he said to Margot when they were back in the hall, 'Can *you* help me at all?'

'Professor Bodkin made a lifetime study of the subject, Professor. I am only his secretary.'

'Hasn't any of his knowledge rubbed off?'

'It's said that a little learning is a dangerous thing.' She almost smiled. 'I know that you are disappointed not to have got any advice on your very unusual story, but I expect Professor Bodkin was most interested in what you told him.'

So were you, thought Guido, and drove away in deep frustration. He had given away his secret to someone who, he felt sure, knew much more than she claimed to know, and gained nothing except acquaintance with another horror.

# CHAPTER THREE

'THE ATMOSPHERE AT HOME is distinctly chilly,' said Kate. 'Dad came home late and Mum didn't like it. And I must say his excuses were pretty lame. He's a rotten liar. The trouble is, Mum tackled me about it. In an off-hand way, you know. Had I noticed anything unusual about Dad's behaviour lately? Well, I had, of course, but I said I hadn't. Then she said, "You've been a little strange yourself lately, Kate. Now tell me the truth, is it anything to do with your father?" I said no, but I'm no match for her, Adam, never have been. Then she seized on something else. Quite hopefully, in fact. Had I fallen out with Adam? I should have said yes, but like a fool I said, "Oh no, Adam's a great help in all this." And she said, "In all what?" I bluffed my way out somehow, but now she's got me worried, because I'm wondering if I've got it all wrong after all and he's not worrying about me but about whoever kept him out late.'

'How late was he?' asked Adam.

'About the time it takes to play footsie under a café table,' said Kate morosely.

Adam had always suspected that Kate's elf was imaginary, and now that he had heard this his suspicions were reinforced. His mind devised one of those facile psychological equations we are all fond of making: Kate feared her father's affections were being alienated; her memory went back to a distressing incident in her childhood;

23

consequently she dreamed of elves; this in recollection became an actual vision of one. QED. But with admirable commonsense he disclosed none of this to her. Instead he said:

'He probably wants some time to think, so he's staying on at work.'

'You really think so?'

'It'd be more in character, wouldn't it?'

'You've cheered me up.'

'Have you rung Professor Bodkin yet?'

'He's ex-directory.'

'Oh yes, would be. Have you written to him?'

'Not yet.'

'Better get a move on, then. No, come on. We'll write it together. Now.'


'Oh my *God*!' groaned Guido Crimonesi.

His wife, reading the newspaper at the breakfast table, or pretending to do so, did not respond.

'It's Julia's birthday,' he lamented.

'And you've forgotten it.'

'Yes.' He was going to add, bitterly, that she might have reminded him in time; she always did, but they were not on very good terms just now.

'This is the first time you've ever forgotten it,' she said.

'I'll have to send her a belated present, I suppose.'

But Kate, who had just come in, said, 'No you won't, Dad. I'll take her something from the shop. She collects these porcelain figurines. We've just got one in that she'll like.'

'Oh, Katie, that's marvellous. Will they give you the time off?'

'Oh of course, if it's for a customer. I'm afraid it isn't cheap, Dad.'

'No, it's not,' he said ruefully, when she named the

24

price. 'Never mind, you've saved my life, dear. Can you take a card along with it?'

'Yes, all right. I'll find a nice picture of a cactus.'

Kate was doing this favour to suit herself rather than her father. A chat with Aunt Julia was overdue. Adam was comforting, but she suspected that he was humouring her, and Aunt Julia would certainly not do that.

She collected the figurine and caught the bus to Roydene Crescent where her aunt lived. It came on to rain as she walked from the bus stop, and she arrived at the maisonette gleaming like a seal in her black jacket. Number 23a was the upper half of a divided building, and through the frosted glass of the front door she watched the aberrated figure of Aunt Julia descend the stairs.

'Ah, Caterina,' said Miss Mandible with satisfaction; her birthday was not forgotten after all. 'Come on. Don't drip over everything. Hang that jacket thing up in the kitchen.'

She was tall and thin, with a long narrow face that never completely smiled, although it could register feeling like a cat's ears. A graduate of daunting qualifications, she had taught Guido from the age of five until the age of twelve, when he had gone to England and a public school. His parents had been travelling the world in the pursuit of money, and he was far closer to her than to them. She might have been the indirect cause of his rejecting his religion, for she had been brought up in a convent under preposterous conditions and had a hatred of formal worship, but she had never tried openly to influence him. As for her own beliefs, they were the opposite of his. She took folk-lore seriously and believed more or less unreservedly in superstitions, maintaining that they were relics of ancient wisdom. This seemed curious in so educated a person, but Miss Mandible was unique. Even her name was unique, the only one in the telephone directory.

She did not suffer fools gladly, nor clever people either. She would have hated teaching classes of children but she and Guido got on so well that they might have been twin stalks on one plant, but pointing in different directions. She fostered the calculating brain of her precocious protégé and never imposed her own singular values on him, although they must have been in the air he breathed, like bacteria. He thought her quaint, relied on her in a dozen ways, and took her for granted.

She unwrapped the package that Kate had brought her. It contained the little figure of a ragged old tramp sitting on a park bench, the kind of piece sometimes lightly called Capodimonte, although real Capodimonte is rare. She said, 'Very nice,' but her expression was noncommittal, rather like that of someone who has worked a slot machine and failed to win anything. The ornaments in her small living room were as thick as rooks on a farmer's field: soldiers, shepherdesses, hunters, dancers – good stuff, indeed, Meissen, Royal Doulton, Worcester – but too many. Every time she got a new figurine she hoped, in an unclarified way, for a miracle, and was continually disappointed. Kate was something of a miracle, but you couldn't keep her on a shelf.

'*Very* nice,' she repeated dutifully, gave Kate a small kiss on the brow, and departed, to return with coffee.

'Auntie Julia . . .' began Kate.

'Ah, I thought it wasn't just love of me that brought you here,' said Miss Mandible.

'*Mama mia*,' said Kate – she had a jokey way of using Italian expressions with Miss Mandible – 'is it that obvious?'

'Well?'

'I'm worried about Dad.'

'Do you mean he's worried about you?'

'Well, this is it,' said Kate. 'I wish he were, in a way. I mean I wish that was all I had to worry about.' She gave a hesitant and repetitive account of how her father had come home late and her mother had had suspicions. 'She wasn't exactly *pacing the floor*, but you know, anxious, only she didn't have it out with him, only hinted things and more or less sulked, and he'd made feeble excuses, but Adam said that that was because he was very likely working late and it had nothing to do with another woman, he was worrying about me . . .'

'Oh really,' said Miss Mandible, 'isn't everyone being absurdly secretive? Why don't you talk to him? You could clear it all up in five minutes, I expect.'

'Erm,' said Kate. 'Auntie, do you remember me telling you about seeing an elf in a picture?'

'Yes, I do,' said Miss Mandible, curiously. 'When you were very little. How long ago was that?'

'I was eight.'

'What about it?'

Kate told her. 'I've got a strong feeling he's still there,' she said, 'or his reflection is, but I always draw my curtains while it's still light, or if I get home late I draw them first, in the dark.'

'What a fascinating experience,' said Miss Mandible.

She looked fascinated, too, vastly more impressed than she had been by the figurine. Kate was slightly irritated.

'Well, I'd like him to go and be fascinating somewhere else. I mean, why ever should he stick a picture of himself on my window, like a transfer? Could anyone associate me with elves? Why did he turn up in the first place when I was little? And why come back now? Why me, for God's sake?'

'Yes,' conceded Miss Mandible mildly, 'that is a most interesting question.'

Kate rolled her eyes in a most un-English manner, and sighed. 'Sorry,' said Miss Mandible, 'but surely I'm allowed to be interested, and you can't expect me to unravel it all on the spot, like Sherlock Holmes. Do you know about him, by the way?'

'Vaguely,' said Kate glumly. 'Fiction was never encouraged at home.'

'Nor was fact, except of a limited kind. That reminds me of something that Sherlock Holmes said. He said that once you have eliminated the impossible, whatever remains, *however improbable*, must be the truth. That kind of reasoning ought to appeal to you. Only in this case we have to begin by accepting the impossible and work from there. Yes, I know that goes against the grain,' she added, for Kate was looking grim and resigned, 'but at least I'm taking you seriously.'

'Yes, you are.'

'But where does your father come in?'

'Either he's having an affair or else he's on to me.'

'Oh no, he's not having an affair.'

'Why are you so sure?'

'Because if he were he wouldn't make up feeble excuses, he'd make up good ones. He's very thorough, my Guido. Something that he can't cope with must be worrying him. Why should it have to do with you?'

'We're very close,' muttered Kate.

'Yes you are, and also miles apart. I'm toying with the idea that, your being so close, he might be caught up in some haunting of his own.'

'That's taking the impossible too far,' said Kate.

'Read this, Jasper,' said Margot Croupe.

Jasper Hermitage took the letter and read it like one not used to reading, following its lines with his finger. 'Crimonesi,' he said. 'The man's daughter.'

'Yes. Do you see that it requests a reply to someone called Adam Longfellow, not to her own address?'

'Doesn't want her father to know.'

'Well presumably. I don't care about that. What matters is that more people are getting involved. Adam Longfellow will be a relation or boyfriend, I suppose. Let's hope he's been sworn to secrecy. The question is, do we agree to meet this girl? I say we do,' said Margot, meeting Jasper's troubled eye. 'If we don't, she'll hardly let it rest. You don't know what that could lead to. Psychical researchers, Bodkin-cultists, even the tabloid press poking their noses in. I say meet her.'

'And what shall we tell her?'

'That depends. It's what we ask her, rather. Young girls are very susceptible to our kind of knowledge. I am most curious to know why she has been chosen.'

'Accident?'

'Accidents don't happen. Were there any weeds?'

Margot Croupe asked this singularly inconsequential question with intense seriousness, and Jasper's reply was no less earnest.

'Signs of creeping buttercup by one of the hedges.'

'That must come up.'

'Yes, I'll have a good look round. This rain's not helping.'

'I'll come out with you.'

It was raining hard, but Margot donned wellingtons, a raincoat and a sou'wester and toured the garden with a handfork and trug. Together they ransacked the soil until not the tenderest green infant of a weed remained. Devoutly they did it, Jasper remaining stoically out in the wretched weather all morning, while Margot made repeated forays in between bouts of tending Professor Bodkin, who needed all the attention of a young baby, and all that that implied. This too she carried out with meticulous care, looking continually at his one bright, cognizant eye, and talking briskly but respectfully as she washed him.

'With your permission, Professor, I'm going to invite another visitor. It's the daughter of Professor Crimonesi whom you met the other day. A young girl, about eighteen, I think. She's had experiences similar to her father's. She has sent you this letter.' Margot wedged the Professor about with towels and pillows as if he were some valuable object being packed for transport, and read Kate's letter in her dry, precise voice, watching the eye steadily. 'Do you agree that it's better to tackle this rather than ignore it?' The eye widened and narrowed as if transmitting signals. 'Thank you, sir, I'm glad you agree.'

Margot wrote to Kate, care of Adam Longfellow, that afternoon, spending the rest of the time in visits to the Professor and also to the garden, to which she and Jasper Hermitage paid positively obsessional attention. An observer of her curious activities would have noticed that she did no housework at all, yet the house was immaculate.

Evening came. Jasper Hermitage went off on his bicycle to his own house. Margot drew the living room curtains, although it was still quite light, and hovered over the Professor until she was sure that he was secure and comfortable. She then took a key and went to a room upstairs. It was packed with bookcases so closely that she had to move sideways to pass between them, and the window was boarded up. She found a book, switched off the light, locked the door, and went on tiptoe downstairs. She sat beside a reading lamp and read to him.

> *A nightingale, upon a cedir grene,*
> *Under the chambre wal ther as she lay*
> *Ful loude song ayein the moone shene . . .*

She read fluently, mouthing the mediaeval verse more easily even than she had read Kate's letter.

She had brought down an anthology of fourteenth-century writings, and went on to choose extracts more difficult than the Chaucer: from Wycliff's Bible, *Sir Gawain*, *The Owl and the Nightingale*. She read with all the patience of a mother to a young child who loves to hear a story over and over again.

At ten o'clock she attended to his needs and transferred him, with the strength and skill of a judo champion, to a reclining chair, encased him in pillows until he looked like a doll in its box, and covered him with two blankets. She sat in the dark until she was sure he was sleeping. He was tired with listening and fell asleep very soon. She went out, locking the door, and went into the kitchen. She opened the door into the garden and wedged it ajar, then went up to her room.

It was barely half-past ten when she got into bed and, by some process of self control, immediately fell asleep. At midnight, without the help of an alarm clock, she awoke and lay on her back and listened.

The sounds that she expected began. They were as softly persistent as those of wasps building in a gutter, and they expressed the same swarming, ceaseless activity. Floors, ledges, shelves, cupboards, furniture were being wiped and dusted and polished. She was used to this busy hum by now and could tell by the slightest variation in volume what room downstairs her visitors were in. When it rose to a muted burble she knew that they had reached the stairs. After a few minutes they arrived on the landing and she saw a faint green light pass under her door.

She was always afraid that against all her nightly pre-cautions she had left something unguarded, a mirror un-covered or a particular door open, but tonight as on every night the elfin ritual was completed, the hum of activity ceased, and even the 'live' sensation of their presence was gone. She let another quarter of an hour elapse, went silently downstairs and shut the kitchen door. She had honoured her pact with them and the house was safe for another night.

She looked in on Professor Bodkin, letting just enough

light into the room to make him out. His head had rolled sideways on to a pillow and she saw him in profile. In the half-light he looked immeasurably old. The sagging flesh of his face hung away into the pillow, leaving the exposed side stretched and angular, like the jaw of a pike.

# CHAPTER FOUR

'WEIRD NAMES,' said Adam, studying the letter. 'Hermitage. That sounds like a place, not a person. And Margot Croupe, for God's sake. Mind you, names do sometimes fit people amazingly. Our choir mistress at school was Miss Nightingale.'

'They're slightly sinister,' said Kate. 'I wonder if they do fit?'

'No, I shouldn't think so. This letter isn't a bit sinister.'

Kate turned it towards her on the café table and reread it.

Dear Kate Crimonesi,

Thank you for your very interesting letter. Professor Bodkin is most willing to hear of your unusual experience at first hand.

He will be pleased for you to call at 3 p.m. on the 4th August, if that is convenient to you.

I must tell you that he has had a serious illness which has affected his speech, and will not be able to discuss your case, but I will answer any questions to the best of my ability.

When you arrive here, please wait at the gate, where Mr Hermitage, the Professor's gardener, will meet you and conduct you to the house.

I look forward to meeting you.

Yours sincerely, Margot Croupe (Miss)
SECRETARY TO PROFESSOR BODKIN.

'No, you're right,' said Kate. 'Prissy old maid.'

'Yes. We're to be conducted to the house. In case we run amok and trample a daisy, I suppose.'

'I wonder if this will prove anything.'

'How are things at home?'

'They're going to Italy for a fortnight on Saturday.'

'Oh. Does that mean . . . ?'

'I'm afraid not, Adam. Aunt Julia's coming to stay with me.'

'Oh.'

'Yes, quite. Still, you desert me half the time, playing with your quintet or rehearsing. Anyway I like Aunt Julia.'

'Are your parents getting on all right?'

'Well, Mum's cheered up because now that that vacation course is over they're always together, so she must feel either he was having an affair but has packed it in, or else it was a false alarm, so she wins either way. But as for him, something's still on his mind, and I'm sure it's me, but it's simply not discussable . . . Aunt Julia said something that really got to me. I said Dad and I were very close, and she said yes, and miles apart too. I'd never realized it, but she's right.'

Ever since receiving that awakening Kate had fairly brooded on it. It was true that her mind and her father's were so alike that they could spot the answer to a problem simultaneously; it was true that they loved each other in a deep unexpressed way; but it was also true that he was male and she was female, a truth so obvious that she had never considered it before. She and her mother were not nearly so close, but they were of the same sex, and this elementary fact quite alienated him in many ways.

34

Guido Crimonesi, however, was living on a desert island of his own making. His pride insisted that he had let himself be taken in, but the horror of his experience was growing. The creature itself had been disturbing enough, but worse still had been that heaving carpet of under-growth, that intimation that the wood was packed with monstrous life, made worse, because just before that the wood had seemed a haven of peace. It reminded him of the daunting fact that if you looked at a pair of beloved lips through a microscope, you would find it seething with bacteria. He flattered himself nevertheless that he was keeping all this to himself. He was not, quite.

More than once he had wanted to confide in his sensible wife, but always balked at it.

'Do you remember', he remarked, 'how Katie once said she saw an elf in a photograph?'

'I remember it very well. There was quite a scene. Why did you suddenly think of that?'

'No special reason,' he replied, faint-hearted.

She sensed something amiss in his manner, and gave him a puzzled glance, but she could not put her misgiv-ings into words. He was back to thinking about the rat in human clothes and did not notice. He had at first feared that it would haunt him like the elf in the lecture room, but it never had. There was of course a difference: the elf had been unseen by all but himself and must surely have come from his own mind. The creature in the wood however had been solid flesh, as if something from the picture-book world of his infancy, the world of bunnies in trousers and hedgehogs in pinnies sweeping their doorsteps, had become real and obscene. He kept insisting that he had seen a common rat and imagined the clothes, but he was persuading himself against his will.

' "Enter these enchanted woods, you who dare," ' remarked

Adam, as they drove through a miserable drizzle along Dovecot Lane.

'What's that, some poem?' said Kate.

'That's right, some poem.'

'I'm terribly ignorant. Dad always said that the danger of poetry is that it destroys your sense of science.'

'Yes, and the danger of bloody science is that it destroys your sense of poetry. Although actually . . . Hang on, that's funny.' He drew up beside the little rustic bridge. 'It's not raining in there, do you see?'

'It's the foliage overhead,' said Kate. 'This rain's too fine to penetrate it.'

'Ah, there speaks the voice of science. Let's press on, then.'

'Yes, all right. I'm rather scared, Adam.'

When they arrived at the gate and were about to leave Adam's car, Jasper Hermitage loomed up, hoe in hand. He was wearing a longish coat apparently made of sacking, and an oilskin cap from under which his iron-grey hair sprouted. He looked like a saturnine gravedigger. He glowered at Kate and Adam, hesitated, then turned away and slouched towards the house.

'He didn't like the look of us,' remarked Adam.

'I didn't fancy him, either,'

Margot Croupe came down the path, holding up an umbrella.

'I had expected you would come on your own.'

'Adam drove me here,' said Kate.

'Ah, I see,' said Margot, but she stood there like Horatius on the bridge. Adam said obligingly, 'It's all right, I can just wait here.'

'I would prefer it. I'd ask you in to see the garden –'

'Oh, I'd like that –'

'– only of course it's much too wet. Please come this way – may I call you Kate?'

'Of course,' said Kate wanly, and after a helpless glance at Adam she let herself be taken to the house. Jasper followed, leaned his hoe against the wall, and wrestled with his footwear.

'Walk into my parlour,' thought Adam uneasily. But no, don't imagine trouble. He switched on his car radio, found no music to his taste, and after a few minutes began backing his car down the lane for the sake of something to do.

He stopped beside the rustic bridge, lowered his window, and looked across to where no rain was falling. 'Long live the weeds and the wilderness yet,' he recited to himself, having a bad habit of quoting. And indeed they were very pretty, the convolvulus and dandelions and buttercups and the general entanglement. The place seemed a dry oasis in this wet summer; and on an impulse he left the car and crossed the bridge into the wood.

It was lovely there, so peaceful and so mild. He peered up at the branches overhead for signs of the rain but could neither see nor hear any sign of it. Kate had been wrong, no rain was falling over this wood; it was a freak of nature. He would have liked to explore but the densely packed brambles prevented that, and he found a tree stump not far from the edge and sat down on it. He was tempted to forget his obligation to Kate and remain here, like the lotus eaters in the poem, mooning away the time.

Then the music began.

He heard the faint, sweet, plaintive strains of a distant pipe. Not a flute, he thought; purer, more liquid. Not a tin whistle; not so perky. A pipe made of reeds, perhaps. He had never seen a pipe made of reeds, but it fitted better than any instrument known to him. He wished he had brought his flute and could respond to it. The lilting tune was easy to catch. Too easy; it stuck in the head, with two or three phrases repeated again and again; they became monotonous and then bothersome like insects. He could not get rid of them. Suddenly he sprang up to shake himself free of the tune or rather, he tried to spring up, but found it quite an effort. The tune persisted and was now louder. He did not want any more of it. He felt oddly sluggish walking back to the bridge, but he made it, and got back into his car.

Margot briefed Kate in the hall about the Professor's condition, while Jasper was lugging off his wellingtons in the porch and putting on some sandals. Kate began stammering her story partly to the Professor, with his one keen eye, and partly to his two employees. She was describing how, at the age of eight, she had seen the elf in the photograph and shown it to her father, when Jasper began to say something.

'He –' But Margot interrupted in a flash.

'– did not see it, of course. We learned as much from Kate's letter. Please let her tell us in her own way.'

Kate made a mental note of the interruption and went on with her story. Margot listened as if she had stopped breathing, and when Kate described seeing the elf in profile, and its aged look, she made a barely perceptible movement of increased attention. Jasper, his hands on his knees, stared at the floor, but the Professor kept an unblinking eye on her. It was as though the eye of a dummy had been lit up. Kate could hardly bear to look at him. She finished, slightly flushed. Margot spoke very kindly, but looked continually from Kate to the Professor, as if she were taking her cue from him.

'You told that very well, Kate. You're very intelligent, aren't you? And that's all?'

'Yes, that's all.'

'But you might have seen more, if you hadn't drawn your curtains.'

'I–'

'Oh, I understand, you were scared, naturally enough. But think: scared of what? Your experience was wonderful. Why, it was like an astronomer sighting a new planet. You were amazingly privileged.'

'You want me to look for him again, don't you?' said Kate.

'If you can bring yourself to do so, yes, I'd love to hear about it.'

She was as eager as someone desperate to make a sale.

'What good would it do if I did, Miss Croupe?'

'I may be able to throw some light on it. I typed Professor Bodkin's book, you know. I couldn't help learning a few things.'

'No, it's a long book,' said Kate, and smiled. Margot smiled back.

'You're a very beautiful girl, Kate.'

'Thank you,' said Kate, but she could have dispensed with the compliment. Suddenly, for no reason, she was reminded of something Adam had said: *Don't they carry off little girls?* Oh, come on. She wasn't a little girl. She weighed nine stone. She'd flatten that tiny ethereal figure.

'Kate,' said Margot, 'the young man who brought you here – he knows about this, presumably? Is he discreet?'

'He wouldn't tell his friends about it, if that's what you mean. He'd be afraid of being laughed at.'

'Well that's good. It's most important to keep this to ourselves. On no account do we want vulgar curiosity. This is your personal affair.'

'Yes,' said Kate, 'but why me? Why ever should it be me?'

'Like you, I'm longing to know.'

Kate left, promising secrecy (she had not mentioned Miss Mandible) and Margot Croupe's features resumed their normal lines. Jasper Hermitage rose heavily.

'I don't like it,' he said.

'I like it better now,' said Margot.

'That's a lovely kid,' said Jasper gruffly.

'Charming.'

'Yes, well . . .' muttered Jasper, but left the observation unfinished and slouched from the room. Margot faced the Professor.

'I think she's the one,' she said.

# CHAPTER FIVE

'THE GARDENER was going to say something about my father,' said Kate, 'but the woman cut him off. He must have been going to give something away, or she wouldn't have jumped on him the way she did. I can't imagine what they know about my Dad, but they know something I don't.

'There's something about that Professor, too. He's really weird. If it weren't for one of his eyes you'd think he was dead, but that eye fixes you, it's far from dead, it's eerie. I don't believe he had an ordinary stroke.'

'Mm?' said Adam.

'Although I suppose the doctor did.'

'Oh, yes,' said Adam.

'Sorry if I'm boring you', said Kate, 'or are you just in a trance?'

'Kate, can I tell *you* something? I heard this music –'

'Oh for God's sake,' said Kate.

Adam's tendency to hear music at inopportune times was the chief source of friction between them. It was exasperating to suspect, that when she was murmuring endearments, he was listening not to her but to Mozart in his head. She was pretty sure that he was in love with her, but music was a rival love and one that would last him all his days.

'No, listen,' he said.

He told her what he had heard in the wood. The little

41

tune was not like those snatches of music that visited his mind uninvited and made him absent-minded; this tune bickered away continually, like spring water in the hills.

'Oh yes?' said Kate unsympathetically. She had a lot more to tell him, important stuff, and she felt that he was capping her story with one of his own. Why drag music into this? 'It was probably birdsong,' she said.

'It was like nothing on earth,' said Adam, and his serious-ness impressed her in spite of herself.


'Of course the evidence is very flimsy,' said Miss Mandible.

'It was the way the Croupe woman pounced on him,' said Kate. 'He was going to commit a *faux pas*, I'm sure he was. I've got an idea he's not very bright. He looks all scholarly, but I don't think there's anything behind it. The thing is, he seemed to know something about Dad. I'd almost believe that Dad got in touch with him in some way, but that's impossible, knowing him.'

'It might account for his coming home late that night,' remarked Miss Mandible.

'Oh my God! so it might. But why on *earth* should he –'

'Well, one thing's for certain, he'd keep that hidden,' said Miss Mandible. 'To admit to any dealings with Profes-sor Bodkin would be like a teetotaller confessing to secret drinking. He had no time for fantasy, even when he was five years old. It was rather sad: he loved fairy stories, but he deliberately denied himself, like some poor little thing doing a penance. It was the same with religion; I used to take him to Mass because his parents wished me to, but he set his face against it, and as soon as he could he broke away. Perhaps it was my fault, indirectly; you know what I think about all that. But the trouble was, he rebelled against all things imaginative. Mathematics became his religion. And what's mathematics? It's a system of logic applied to numbers. Oh yes it is, Caterina—' (Kate frowned an objection) '—it's that and no more. Just think about it. Of course, astronomy filled this gap for him to some extent. Astronomy is full of wonder. But I've always thought he liked the spaces between the stars better than the stars themselves.'

'Auntie Julia,' said Kate, 'I'm frightened of that woman.'

'Why, Caterina?'

'She was so desperate to get me involved. I wish I'd never gone to see her. But then I am involved. I don't know whether to move or stick. What if he gets tired of being curtained off and comes looking for me? And it's not just me. Dad's in it, God knows how. And Adam. I was nasty to him, but I know he heard something. Why Adam? What's he done to deserve it?'

'The legends', remarked Miss Mandible, 'are full of cases of people being bewitched by music. Adam has a very keen ear for it.'

'Oh he certainly has, if you scrape your knife on your plate he'll say "That's E flat", but you can't say that elves only pick on people who're sympathetic to them. What about me? I'm the last person for them to favour, with my upbringing.'

'Or perhaps you only think you are. Caterina, do you think I'd see this phenomenon if I watched with you? No, don't put me off. It looks as if this Miss Croupe wants to monopolize you, in which case you need an ally. Besides, I don't like being left out.'

Adam and his quintet played regularly at a *thé dansant*, rendering innocuous tunes innocuously, while the customers chattered, ignored them, and then acknowledged them with languid clapping. When he gave a solo they would clap him with rather more feeling, because he commanded attention; he could make the most hackneyed tune ripple with arabesques. This evening he played 'The

Londonderry Air', which can hardly spring surprises, but a hush fell on his listeners. Spoons and forks ceased clattering. Waitresses communicated with their customers with silent gestures. When he finished, no one clapped at first. The silence was uncomfortable. Adam sat down. His fellow players glanced curiously at him. Then the clapping burst out as if with relief, and he rose and bowed to it. Conversation burst out too, and he overheard scraps of it, praising him, but he knew that their praise was uneasy. He had managed to lend the blandest of tunes a peculiar overtone, rather sinister, and everyone felt rather as Kate had when the elf had turned its pretty face and looked old.

Everyone supposed that he was enthralled by the music, rapt in it. The contrary was true. He had hardly known what he was playing. He had gone through the famous tune mechanically, ruled by another. It was at the back of his mind all the time, and he went about as if expecting an ambush.

Kate was sorry that she had not taken him seriously.

'Play me something, Adam,' she said, as she sat with him in his bedsit.

'Why?' This was not her usual way of passing time in his bedsit.

'Because I want you to.'

He played 'Humoresque', that piece much favoured by musical novitiates. This sprightly tune ends with a tender little trill, pleasing to the ear, but this time it was as if some mocking undersong were humming behind the notes. Kate had little feeling for music, unlike her father, and she wished she had not asked him to play. At the same time she was provoked into asking him for more.

'Play me what you heard in the wood.'

He gave her an interrogative stare.

'Go on,' she said. 'Let's share it.'

But when he raised the flute to his lips she was seized

44

with misgivings and stayed his arm. She had never cared to *watch* him play; it pulled his face into unbecoming grimaces. But this time it was as if there were a face behind the face, and it frightened her.

'No, no don't,' she cried. 'Don't, don't!'

Kate pulled her curtains to, switched on her table lamp, arranged two chairs at the table, undressed, put on a dressing gown, and called Miss Mandible into her bedroom. She drew her curtains back, and they sat side by side, reflected five times in the bay window. Miss Mandible was impassively expectant; as if she were about to hear the lesson read in church. But nothing happened. Their twin reflections looked back at them, unaccompanied, from all five panes. Kate felt disappointed and foolish. She shifted about, coughed. She was reflected shifting about and coughing.

Miss Mandible said, 'Can you sense anything at all, Kate?'

'Nothing.'

'Oh well,' said Miss Mandible, stoically, for there was no doubt that she felt let down, 'it's a law of life that when you want something to happen it won't. Another time, perhaps.'

'Yes, all right.'

Kate drew her curtains and paced about her room again alone. She had lost faith in herself; she wondered if she were simply inducing well-intentioned people into humouring her. What had Margot Croupe actually *said* except that she was interested? Adam? He might even be having sympathy pains like an expectant father. Oh no, this was becoming ridiculous. She opened her curtains again.

'Come on,' she said, 'prove me wrong. I mean right.'

But, not to tempt disappointment further, she went to switch off her table lamp, and as her reflection in the central pane bent over, something else drifted into shape beside it. At first it was too indistinct to be defined. It was not the elf. It was a face. It was the face of an old, old man. One of its eyes was blank and unseeing, but the other glared and oscillated. Kate swayed and gripped the edges of her table for support. The movement of her reflection seemed to disturb the image beside it, like a stone making ripples in water. The face dissolved and reformed into the figure of the elf in profile, hard and pitiless as stone. It turned its head and became pretty, poisonously pretty.

This was like a dream, with its images shifting and melting, but only like one; this was *not* a dream. Kate was awake and conscious. She could have recited her seven times table. After feeling faint for a moment she felt calm enough to outface the coy figure in the window, and she did indeed stare at it until it vanished.

She closed her curtains yet again, went slowly and deliberately to her table, and switched off the lamp. Then panic rushed in upon her and she dashed for her door.

'Aunt Julia!' she shouted. 'Aunt Julia!'

Miss Mandible insisted on moving Kate into her own bedroom, Kate's parents' bedroom. To save her from sharing the double bed she dismantled the single bed in the third bedroom and made Kate lug it in with her. Kate did so, protesting. She was now feeling merely irritable, uncertain as to whether she was really being persecuted, like someone receiving obscene phone calls, or whether her imagination, held in check so long, was at last running wild.

'There's no need for this,' she said crossly, as they reassembled the bed.

'Well, I think there is. I mean to keep an eye on you, Caterina.'

'I'm probably just mad.'

'If you are, all the more reason to keep an eye on you.'

'It'll be impossible to get at the dressing table with this bed in the way,' said Kate petulantly.

'We'll have to kneel up on it.'

Miss Mandible's calm hid feelings that Kate could not have guessed at. She had longed to see the elf in the window; it would have made her in an indefinable way a part of Kate's young world. Guido, the joy of her life, had grown apart from her. He had a wife and daughter; the daughter had a boyfriend; and she, Miss Mandible, had a collection of porcelain figurines. Contact with a creature from the realms of legend would fill a spiritual gap, but she seemed doomed to be the eternal counsellor while the young ones got the action. Even harrowing action would be better than no action at all.

Kate rose early the next morning, took Aunt Julia a cup of tea and left her aunt to conduct her toilet in decent privacy, while she had breakfast. A letter dropped on the mat while she was doing so. *Miss Crimonesi* was written on the envelope; no address, no stamp. The writing was copperplate, so perfect that no expert could have deduced character from it. The message inside was on a postcard in the same beautiful hand.

Dear Miss Crimonesi,

Do not go any further in this matter. It is dangerous, very very dangerous.

It was unsigned.

Guido Crimonesi's trip to Italy was a duty rather than a pleasure. He and his wife were staying with his parents, now in their seventies and retired, at their villa outside the town of Baveno in the northern lake district. The elder Crimonesis were disappointed in their son. The cleverest of their children, he could have been a successful banker or stockbroker, with his head for figures; instead he had chosen to lead the relatively poverty-stricken life of a university lecturer. And he was so hurtfully cold. The Crimonesis, although they had left him in the charge of a governess at the age of five, and sent him to a school in England at the age of twelve, believed passionately in family life and revelled in demonstrations of affection. He was not grateful for their love. In truth Guido would have loved to return it, but found it impossible. He loved others instead, after his fashion. He had always been content with this, and prided himself on being more English than the English. But now, in the sultry Italian air and under family pressure, he began to doubt himself. He was seriously worried that he might have been false to his true nature, and that it was having its revenge by making him see phantom elves and rats in human clothing.

He tried to disguise his worries by being friendly and jolly and laughing a lot. His parents merely thought that he had adopted English manners, but his wife was alarmed and convinced that he was not well. Indeed, he was not. His nights were disturbed by dreams. He spent bleak tracts of the night in hollow wakefulness, interspersed with dreams in which he heard himself groaning and muttering. Sometimes, in the moment between sleeping and waking, the elf would alight on the end of his bed and begin to crawl towards him, bringing its smirking face almost up to his pillow. Once he swiped at it and cried, 'Get away, damn you!', to the consternation of his wife. Sometimes the rat-headed creature would appear, bringing a multitude of its friends, and they would encircle him, their numbers ever increasing, until there were heaving masses of them. Sometimes he would be in Professor Bodkin's cottage, watched by the secretary, who grinned at him, her eye-teeth showing like fangs, while the

Professor himself slowly stirred and began to leave his chair like a corpse coming to life. Guido tossed and turned and jabbered broken words and phrases, and was in the very throes of this when he awoke suddenly one morning in brilliant Italian sunshine. His wife was sitting up in bed staring at him with a blend of accusation and concern.

'Guido,' she said, 'who is Margot Croupe?'

# CHAPTER SIX

'HOW DOES HE MEAN "dangerous", I wonder?' mused Kate.

Adam picked up the postcard again. 'The gardener bloke wrote this I suppose.'

'Well, I didn't think it came from the borough council,' said Kate, irritated.

'I only meant he hadn't signed it. What did you make of him?'

'Thick.'

'Hmm. If he's a qualified gardener he's not thick. They have to know all those Latin names. I wonder why he didn't sign it. Scared to commit himself, I suppose. We ought to follow it up. Ask him what he's on about.'

'That woman would see us.'

'I don't suppose he lives in. Most unlikely. Let's look him up. Hermitage, wasn't it?' Adam left his bedsit and went down to the hall, to return with a telephone directory. 'Luckily it's a rare name. Good God, there are three of them. Hermitage A., dentist. No, I shouldn't think so. Hermitage J., 14 Arden Place. And there's Hermitage W., 27 Bryden's Lane.'

Adam rang Hermitage, W., and asked if that was Mr Hermitage, the gardener at Dovecot Lane. He was told that he had got the wrong number. He then made Kate write a note to Mr J. Hermitage to say that she was greatly concerned at his warning and needed most urgently to see him, and would be calling at eight o'clock that evening. They found Arden Place in the street directory, delivered the note, and felt a little better for it.

'What does your all-knowing aunt think of this?' asked Adam, as they drove away.

'My all-knowing aunt is all for getting in on the act herself. At least I think so. I sensed she was miffed at not seeing the elf – she's always taken fairies seriously. I used to think that was just her little foible but now look what's happened to me.'

'But what does she *say*?'

'Nothing specific, except that you can't trust elves. They're like deadly nightshade, pretty but poisonous.'

'So is their music,' said Adam.


Mrs Crimonesi listened patiently as Guido shamefacedly told her about a little green man and a rat in leggings and a jerkin, but her feelings were mixed.

She was relieved: Guido could not have had an affair, or he would have made up a much better story than this. She was even amused: it was ironical that Guido, who dismissed religion as the superstition of the immature, should be seeing creatures from the nursery. But she was also alarmed; because this shed a disturbing light on his relationship with Kate.

Oh, it was perfectly healthy, of course, an intellectual camaraderie, but beneath it there was a deep, strong bond which meant they were of supreme importance to each other. With Guido, Kate came first, last and in the middle. The child had probably held the marriage together, but she would have preferred her own powers to have done that.

Ten years ago Kate had imagined that she had seen an elf in a picture. And now it seemed Guido had seen it too! They were that close. They were like those identical twins who, so she had heard, share each other's thoughts and feelings. And now after ten years he was seeing it again, with complications. What to make of it?

People in the past would have consulted magicians. Mrs Crimonesi resorted, in the modern manner, to amateur psychology. Kate was soon to go to university. Mothers are sometimes upset by the separation. Fathers, more often, are simply pleased with a goal achieved. But Guido was a special case. He was glad that Kate had done well, of course, but inside he must be dismayed at the thought of losing her to the world. Suppressed emotions were giving him bizarre illusions, so the sensible Mrs Crimonesi reasoned, while her husband told his tale.

She suggested rest, perhaps a psychiatric consultation, and certainly no more visits to that woman with the ridiculous name.

'Brenda,' said Guido anxiously, 'you won't tell Katie about this, will you?'

'Of course not,' said Brenda, resolving to do so at the earliest opportunity.

Arden Place was a dingy cul-de-sac with a row of terraced houses down one side and a row of garages, suggestive of public lavatories, down the other. Kate had half-imagined that the gardener, with a name like Hermitage, would live in a hut in the depths of the wood, and she feared that despite their detective work some quite irrelevant face might poke itself out of number 14. Doubts were dispelled, however, when Jasper's own beetling features appeared in the doorway.

He hurried them inside as if they were fugitives from the law, shut the door, and turned to them in the hall, which was occupied by his bicycle, and was so narrow that they had to stand in single file.

He looked so unwelcoming that Kate was moved to say, 'If you didn't want us to come you shouldn't have written

53

to me, Mr Hermitage. It was the surest way of bringing me here. Did you think I'd just say "OK, I'll drop it then."? Curiosity alone wouldn't let me do that.'

'Yes,' said Jasper, still blocking the narrow hallway. 'I should have known this would happen. I suppose I hoped I'd frighten you off. But it's no use your tracking me down like this. I can't give you any explanations. I'm as much in the dark as you are. I know what's going on, up to a point, but I can't tell you why. I can't put it too strongly, *don't* ask why, *don't* ask for explanations, it's the worst thing you could do. You're not so far in that you can't turn back. Professor Bodkin asked too hard, and look what happened to him. I don't meddle with things any more than I can help, and neither should you.'

'Then why do you go on working there, Mr Hermitage?' demanded Kate. 'Aren't there plenty of other gardens to work in?'

Jasper looked sternly at Kate, making her lower her eyes. 'I do what I must,' he said finally. 'You might say I'm under a spell, if you think that way, but don't think that way, don't think at all. See now, I've given you my advice. Don't do anything, forget it.'

'They won't forget us, Mr Hermitage,' said Adam. 'Kate keeps seeing things and I keep hearing music.'

'*Music?* You heard music? Where? In the wood? You went into the wood and you heard music?'

'That's right, music,' said Kate impatiently. She didn't care for Jasper's attention to be so completely diverted to Adam. But Jasper ignored her. 'Are you musical?' he asked. 'Play an instrument, do you?'

'I am a musician,' said Adam, somewhat self-importantly.

Jasper brooded on this, like a barrister in court who is suddenly presented with new evidence. Then without a word he motioned them into his living room. It contained a bare wooden table which bore the remains of a meal, two upright chairs, and a shabby armchair beside the small fireplace. A tatty carpet was fringed with bare boards. There was a one-bar electric fire in the grate. On the mantelpiece there was the photograph of a woman: middle-aged, with gold-rimmed glasses, and permed hair. 'The wife,' said Jasper, noticing Kate's glance. 'Walked out on me. You couldn't blame her. Couldn't stand living with Them.' He offered her the armchair with a gesture; she sank lower than him and Adam, on the other two chairs, and felt at a disadvantage. Jasper turned again to Adam.

'So you're in this too. Tell me what happened.'

Adam told him: the strange weather in the wood, the elfin music. 'Ah yes,' he said, 'they know how to get at you, they go to where your heart is, to where your treasure lies . . .'

Kate, resentful at being left out, protested, 'That doesn't apply to me at all!', but Jasper still did not heed her. 'They get at you where you're strong, because that's also where you're weakest,' he said. 'You must just stop listening, young man.'

'That's impossible!' exclaimed Adam; but Kate didn't want him to agonize over his own problem, and fairly forced herself into the conversation. 'But are they real, Mr Hermitage?' she demanded. 'You make it sound as if they were something we wanted to imagine, but I can't see how that applies to me –'

'Are they real? That's a philosopher's question. Professor Bodkin might know, but he asked too hard. I don't know, I'm right out of my depth. I tell you, I can't put it too strongly, don't let them be real, shut them out, forget them. I know it sounds hard, but you can do it if you want to.'

'Well anyway,' said Kate, keeping a determined eye on Adam, who was smouldering in silence. 'Miss Croupe didn't tell me to forget it. She wants to hear more.'

And now Jasper did turn his full attention to Kate. He looked around as if afraid of being overheard, and spoke in a low voice.

'Miss Croupe wants to use you.'

Kate was chilled, and it made her manner calm and accusing. 'Oh does she? In what way? Is she going to make an image of me and stick pins in it?'

'Miss Croupe is a very good woman,' said Jasper solemnly. 'She is a dedicated woman. She's a clever woman, a scholar. She has devoted her life to Professor Bodkin. She was his student. Then his secretary. She spent years with him on that book. And all the other books. Books, books, books. They lost themselves in them. I mean it, lost themselves. Burrowed in them . . . All locked away now. Every book he ever touched. Dangerous now. Like the weeds in the garden . . .' Kate was knitting her brows in perplexity, for Jasper was now rambling, but he went on, speaking as much to himself as to her. 'She reads him bits of his old books every night. Rations him as if they were drugs.' He looked up at Kate and became conscious of her again. 'And she nurses him, of course. You realize what that means. No, Miss Croupe is not a witch, she's more like a saint; you never saw such self-sacrifice. But there it is, you see. She doesn't mind sacrifice. She's ready to sacrifice you.'

Kate was shaken afresh, but she still would not show it. 'She'd do better getting in a specialist,' she said. 'A stroke can be treated.'

'It wasn't a stroke,' said Jasper.

But before Kate could challenge this, with its ominous hint of 'a spell', Adam burst in:

'You can't just leave it at this! I mean, you say stop listening, how am I to do that?'

'Up to you.'

'Yes, but, you mean, give up playing?'

'Adam,' said Kate, 'you're not the only one in this, you know.'

Adam looked away with troubled eyes. Jasper summed both of them up in a glance, and stood up.

'I don't mean to be rude, but I don't want to prolong this,' he said. 'I've taken a risk discussing it at all.'

Kate turned as they left the hall.

'You're a strange sort of gardener, Mr Hermitage.'

'I keep a strange sort of garden,' said Jasper.

Only when they had left did Kate, to her chagrin, remember the questions she had left unasked. One concerned what Hermitage knew about her father, the slightest hint of which he had given before Margot Croupe stopped him; and the other was what Hermitage made of the appearance of Professor Bodkin's face at her window. Nervous tension, Hermitage's maddening reluctance, and his frightening references to Margot, had distracted her, but so had Adam's fretting over his own problems. He had diverted Hermitage's attention. He had fairly taken over! As they drove away, in an uncomfortable silence, it was Adam who occupied her thoughts, and not affectionately either.

He was easy-going and good-natured, she reflected, because it suited him. Anything like a bloody battle to the death would distract his attention from his music, and nothing must be allowed to do that. So he fell in with the wishes of his friends and his girlfriend and made himself popular, but if a musical engagement clashed with a social one he would, in the nicest, most disarming way put it first, and if his musical progress were threatened he would pick up his flute and run. All that supportive stuff – 'I'll go with you' – 'We'll write the letter together' – 'We ought to sort it out not quarrel' – didn't count for much in the end. Music always won.

They drove without a word to Kate's house. Adam drove

very courteously, allowing other cars the right of way, smilingly signalling to pedestrians to cross, and all to prove, thought Kate, how fair, how considerate he was. When they stopped she said, in a tone that invited refusal, 'Are you going to come in for a while?'

'No, I don't think so, Katie. Better get on.'

'You're fed up with this, aren't you?'

'No, of course not, but –'

'No of course not *but* you're showing every sign of it.'

'I don't know what you're getting at.'

'Well I'll tell you. You don't think I'm safe to know any more, do you? Go around with me and the gremlins get into your playing. Keep away from me and they might go away.'

'It's impossible to talk to you in this mood.'

'Oh no it isn't, I'm listening. Go on, talk.'

'Katie, look. We've got to be reasonable. That Hermitage bloke knows what he's talking about. He kept saying, "Leave well alone". For God's sake, Katie, he couldn't put it clearer, he says it's dangerous to push it any further. Well look, a couple of months and we'll both be at university, away from all this, plenty of other things to distract us. Isn't it common sense to cool it for a bit? Stirring it up the way we're doing must make things worse. What did he say? "You mustn't think of them." We don't think of anything else.'

'Is that it?' said Kate.

'Well, as I say –'

Kate left the car and shut the door very gently.

'Goodbye Adam.'

'*Kate . . .*'

She let herself in, still gently and with care, and made for her own room, but of course was intercepted by Miss Mandible.

'Well?'

'I'll tell you in the morning.'

'Oh, come now, I've been on tenterhooks all evening –'

'I'm very tired. Really. Anyway it was nothing. An anti-climax. He was an old fool. Sorry Auntie. Goodnight.'

Her tears began to drop into the washbasin in the bathroom, and no towelling would dry them. She made a dash for her room to avoid any meeting with her aunt. She drew her curtains with fury, as if to say 'There! Don't try any tricks on me tonight!' She sat for a while, half-dressed, fearing a tap on her door, but none came, and although this was what she wanted, the fact that none came made her feel rejected and deserted. She buried her face into her pillow and cried in rage and misery, she cried till her body was shaken and racked. Then she washed in the basin in her room, drank some water, blew her nose, got into bed, and lay there trying to be reasonable.

She told herself that in a world plagued with strife and outrage, civil war, domestic violence, pollution and famine, she ought not to be fretting about elves or snivelling over boyfriends. But she did not convince herself, because we are always more concerned with our own toothache than with other people's earthquakes. Besides, she mattered to herself and her situation was pretty serious, whatever the state of things in Colombia or Somalia. She thought of Adam and *his* situation, not sympathetically but with a kind of desolate resentment. Even when he was haunted it had to be by music.

# CHAPTER SEVEN

A DAM SAT IN HIS LONELY BEDSIT, which tonight was lonelier than the North Pole, and resented Kate. For someone of such vaunted intelligence she was insanely unreasonable. He had tried hard enough, God knew, to make their relationship run smoothly. He'd listened to her patiently, he'd soothed her fears, he'd cheered her up; with no concern for himself he had persuaded her to write to Professor Bodkin, taken her to see him, hunted for Jasper's address, taken her there, and had throughout been quite nobly supportive. His reward was to be accused of being selfish, and all because he had simply suggested that it might not be a bad idea to take Jasper's advice! Jealousy was at the heart of it. She was jealous of his music, and it showed even in little jokes about what flute-playing did to his face. And when – all for her sake – he had let himself get involved in this humiliating business, she showed no sympathy, but positively blamed him for it.

But then, with the see-saw motion of true love, Adam's feelings began to tilt him towards self-reproach. He'd been tactless. Naturally Kate was terribly uptight and he should have let her hold centre stage until she had time to consider him. Even then he should have been self-effacing, no no, don't worry about me, *you're the one who matters* . . . That was how to stay in her favour. But the bleak fact was that Kate, as she shut the car door, had sounded terribly final. *Goodbye, Adam.* She'd meant it all right, and she had a proud unyielding spirit. His heart sank. And sank.

He wanted to phone her, but it was now late. Anyway the phone was in the hall, his landlady would hear him, and the call would be answered by Kate's formidable aunt. He went to bed, but not to sleep. Kate's words repeated themselves again and again: *You're fed up with this, aren't you? You want out, don't you?* Their scorn knocked the stuffing out of him, and justify himself as he might, he felt demeaned and depleted.

The next morning he was tempted to call on her in the china shop, but refrained, visualizing Kate snootily shifting out of reach as he tried to talk to her, the manageress, hard as nails, watching him with suspicion, and idiots leading cosy unstressed lives constantly interrupting to buy china. At ten o'clock he had a rehearsal, and took himself to the Band Hall (alternatively used as a Scout Hut), glad of something to do.

And instead of Kate there was the music itself to worry about. They were practising sweetish tunes of no particular character for a restaurant, the next thing to piped music, the sort of stuff the quintet could do – and all but did do – in their sleep. But again mockery got into Adam's playing. The smooth notes, with their derisive overtones, did not go unnoticed. After the rehearsal the pianist said: 'You sold your soul to the devil, Adam?'

'I tried to but he chucked it back,' said Adam making a joke of it, but he was worried. He knew he was playing brilliantly, but the brilliance was eerie. He felt cursed.

He played at the restaurant at lunch time, and well into the afternoon, and after each solo there was that brief silence, as if something improper had been said, and then the nervous applause. When it was over he hurried away without a word. And now what? A Kateless evening stretched before him.

He stopped his car in a lay-by, unsure of where to go

next. The traffic swished by, each vehicle slightly rocking his car as it passed, and this became rhythmic like a drum. He was tired from playing after a sleepless night, and was swayed by the rhythm. The elfin tune grew louder in accompaniment to the drumming, and sounded almost like a voice: *come away*, it insisted, *come away, come away* . . . He came to with a jerk and found himself sweating. He knew vaguely that elves and their kind could lure people to their doom, like the will-o'-the-wisp, and the sirens, half women and half birds, and all those other seducers who bait helpless mortals. He must keep awake! Still woozy, he did not trust himself to drive away, but opened his window and took some deep breaths. But this served to increase the hypnotic state, and the music, with its *leit motif* of *come away*, became more insistent still.

He was in Dovecot Lane beside the rustic bridge. He felt no surprise; it seemed natural that he should be here. Ah, there was his car, parked a little way along. He was standing at the brink of the wood, about to go in. But someone was coming towards him down the lane, wobbling on a bicycle. It was Hermitage, and his face wore a triumphant and hideous leer. Adam braced himself, for Hermitage was riding straight at him. But then he was wobbling so much that he must fall off, and did so in earnest, sprawling on the grass verge, making no effort to rise. Adam went up to him and found that he was streaming with blood. There were wounds on his face, his neck, his throat, his hands; they were visible through the torn clothes all over his body. He was in desperate need of help and yet Adam was powerless to move. He felt inadequate, just as he had before Kate's scorn. Hermitage looked up at him, still with that ghastly leer on his mutilated face, and said in an ugly voice, 'I took a risk talking to you.'

Adam asked, foolishly, 'Why are you bleeding?'

*'The elves have teeth, I suppose.'*

And then, without apparently rising and mounting, Jasper was away on his bike, leering at Adam over his shoulder.

Adam was back at the rustic bridge. He felt impelled to enter the wood. He was drawn there by an insistent rushing noise like a swiftly moving torrent. Once inside the wood, he realized that this was caused by thousands of small bodies. The dense undergrowth heaved and crackled with them. And then they burst up all round him, diminutive human forms with the heads of animals: rats, ferrets, squirrels, cats; slithering, leaping, rushing. They collided with him and threatened to engulf him, but they were not concerned with him; they were tearing through the wood in one direction. He stood still as wave after wave of them swept past; he saw them swarm into the water that separated the wood from the cottage garden and make an undulating bridge across it; he saw them attack the house, blackening its walls with their numbers like ants. He heard a woman's voice screaming in agony and terror.

A voice sounded in his ear. It was repeating something forcefully. He blinked, started, and looked out of his car window to see a car trailing a caravan that had hardly been towed clear of the roadway.

'Excuse me. Would you mind moving forward?'

'Oh, sure. OK.'

He drove to the end of the lay-by, got out of his car, and went up to the other driver.

'Sorry about that,' he said in a slurred voice. 'Thanks for waking me. Thanks a lot.'

The other driver looked at him dispassionately. 'I should sleep a bit longer if I were you,' he said. 'Sleep it off.'

The Crimonesis returned, and Miss Mandible, laden with gifts from Italy and the duty free shop, prepared to return to her maisonette. She was asked, 'Everything been all right?'.

'Yes, all in order,' she replied, not to betray Kate's confidence. She flattered herself that she would make a good poker player. Brenda Crimonesi took stock of her and Kate, and said to herself, 'Something between those two.'

In the early days of her marriage she had been jealous of Julia's influence over Guido. She more than replaced his parents and in some ways she upstaged his wife. As the years went by Brenda was consoled by the idea that Julia was superannuated. Guido patronized his old teacher, taking her tremendous intellectual tutelage for granted and tut-tutting good-humouredly over her ludicrous superstitions. But after Guido's alarming confessions during their holiday, Brenda was suspicious and jealous all over again.

Who was it who said, 'Give me the child until the age of seven, and I shall have him for life', or words to that effect, meaning that what a child learns in infancy is never forgotten? Julia had often affectionately recalled how she had plied Guido with fairy stories and how he, a five-year-old sceptic, had refused to be taken in. Was that the root of his trouble? Had he, unconsciously, been taken in all too easily? And now that he was disturbed by the prospect of parting with Kate, were the goblins of his infancy surfacing to torment him? This was Brenda's second theory about Guido's madness, and she had to stretch a point to make it fit the first one, but psychological guesswork will always do that.

She tackled Kate at the earliest opportunity. As she unfolded the tale of Guido's various hallucinations and his visit to 'a woman named, you're not going to believe this, Kate, *Margot Croupe*', Brenda saw her daughter's olive-skinned face go pale. Kate was defenceless now.

'*O mio Dio*,' she muttered.

'We'll speak English if you don't mind,' said Brenda.

'I know just how Dad feels.'

A new idea occurred to Brenda. 'Kate! Are you on drugs?'

She had already dismissed this idea as impossible in Guido's case, but Kate was fresh from sixth form college, and to be experimenting with drugs at her age was all too possible. Brenda's mind made a wild jump at an explanation. Was it possible, just possible, that Guido had learned about it and had joined her out of misguided sympathy?

'Darling,' she said, 'you can tell me. I went to college in the Sixties, you know. I do know about the drug scene. I'm not going to come the heavy parent. I want to help. Tell me, *are* you?'

'*No*, I'm *not*.'

'That's what they all say, you know.'

'Do they? Listen, Mum, you're not going to believe this, but . . .'

Brenda listened. When she had heard it all she said, with a strange sort of stubbornness, 'It still sounds so much like a drug trip to me.'

My God, thought Kate, she'd actually *prefer* me to be on drugs rather than face this. I know just how her mind works. She thinks Dad and I have some weird telepathic link and she hates that.

'Mum, it's the truth. Please believe me.'

Brenda said, spitefully and unreasonably, for she was very upset, 'That woman is a very bad influence on you.'

'What woman? Aunt Julia? Oh my God, you'd throw anyone to the wolves, wouldn't you?'

'When I hear a farrago of nonsense like this I think I'm entitled to–' began Brenda angrily, but stopped, for Kate had burst into tears, and Kate's tears, although extremely rare, could become a monsoon.

A gardening enthusiast would have noticed that Professor Bodkin's garden had no compost heap, nor would he have found any trace of fertilizer. He would have observed that a bonfire was kept burning ceaselessly.

Jasper Hermitage tended the garden like a house-proud woman: weeding, weeding, weeding, and burning the weeds. He banned compost heaps and fertilizers because they nourished weeds. Like Margot Croupe, he had a profound dread of weeds.

He knew that the wood, across the narrow strip of water behind the garden, was haunted by two communities. There were the elves: they had a code of behaviour quite different from our own, but they were prepared to live in harmony with humans provided that they kept strictly to a set of rules. And there were the other ones. They lived in the tangled undergrowth under the trees. They constantly spied on the garden and the cottage but they dreaded a well-tended space and would not venture out of hiding unless there was undergrowth enough to encourage them. And so Jasper and Margot maintained a total war on all weeds with the neurotic intensity with which some people take precautions against disease. It was a war which would never end, and it had ruined Jasper's life.

He had applied for this job a little over ten years ago, when the Professor was still active and at the height of his fame and Margot Croupe was dealing with masses of mail. He was not the best qualified applicant – it was a time of high unemployment and he was up against dozens of others – but Professor Bodkin took to him and Margot Croupe approved. Jasper was a deeply humble man with a feudal sense of loyalty, and he could be relied on to do as he was told. He worked like a beaver and he kept out idle callers. The job was well paid and for a while he was happy, but the atmosphere of the place began to get him down. It was uncanny, a perpetual sense of presences. He was not good with words and could not even begin to describe it, but it gradually turned him from a quiet, contented man to a sullen, suspicious one. His wife, who had lived with him for years in good-natured habit, found his mood unbearable and begged him to change his job. He promised to do so more than once but always put it off.

And then one afternoon some years ago an extraordinary storm broke. There was no sound or anything to see, but it was as if some mounting pressure had surpassed its full extent and burst. He had dashed to the cottage and stared through the living room window to see the Professor struck helpless and Margot Croupe busying herself as if she had trained for this emergency and was practised in all the necessary moves. A doctor was called, an ambulance was summoned and the Professor was taken to hospital. A severe stroke was diagnosed. When Jasper returned home he declared that that was it, he was finished with that damned place, he was leaving without notice. He found that he could not. No explanations: he simply could not. His wife expostulated and stormed and pleaded and wept and sulked. Life at home was hell for a while. When he came back one night to find that she had left, it was a relief.

As for his work, custom made it tolerable. He and Margot were thrown together and a tacit understanding grew between them. He helped her move all the books and cover all the reflecting surfaces and boarded up certain windows for her. He knew that she had strange visitors at certain times. He asked no questions. In so far as the intellectual gulf between them allowed, they became friends.

He knew that Margot worshipped Professor Bodkin and was waiting with that inhuman patience of hers for the circumstances to arise in which he would be released from his spell. Jasper had an idea, all the more horrible for being vague, of what this would involve. He did all that she asked him to, he remained her loyal ally, but this idea troubled him to his depths.

Margot Croupe moved through the days as if she had been

programmed to do so. She so timed her movements that she could pretty nearly say where she would be and what she would be doing at any given minute. She was abnormally withdrawn. People had long since ceased trying to call on her or ask her out. She was to be seen in the supermarket once or twice a week and would nod civilly to 'goodmornings', but she went straight from the checkout to her car without a glance to the left or right. The community at large, if it considered her at all, supposed vaguely that she drove back to a home somewhere over the edge of the world.

She had become a student of Professor Bodkin in 1951, when she was eighteen and he was forty. She buried herself in work, did brilliantly, became a research fellow in the university, and was thrown more and more into the company of Professor Bodkin, whose assistant she became. He was her ideal man, because in the common sense of the word he was not a man at all, he was a reader. Reading with him was not a substitute for living, it was a life in itself. It suited Margot down to the ground, and she worshipped him.

The Professor, in time, became engrossed in myth and folklore. This was not so much a study as a total immersion, like a baptism. His colleagues were embarrassed at first to hear him refer to gnomes, imps, bogles and fairies as if they were living things, but when they discovered that he was writing a story book about them, it put him in the same class as Hans Christian Andersen and Lewis Carroll and made everything all right. *The Gnomes of Yggsdragarth* was a fabulous success and they boasted about their friendship with him. He'd brought these beings to life! He'd even invented a language for them! Only Margot Croupe knew that the book was not fabulous at all, it was a factual record, and the Professor hadn't invented the language; he had learned it. She knew by now that he was privileged, and had insights not granted to ordinary people. She also knew that he needed care. She began to watch over him – his nurse as well as his partner. He retired from teaching and she went to live with him in Dovecot Lane. They hired Jasper and for a while life ran smoothly. Margot began to hope that the Professor had exorcized his obsession through his book and was now truly retired. But then, after she had gone to bed, she would hear him talking to the elves.

Margot listened fearfully, for she was sure that he had gone too far. *How* far gradually dawned on her. The elves needed the Professor's mind in the same way that a parasite needs a host. They had existed in spirit form since time began, but to gain earthly shape they needed human co-operation and they had been deprived of this since the days of the old magicians. For long they had lain dormant because modern man was concerned with science and technology, estranged from their world. Professor Bodkin had rediscovered this world and opened his mind to them, and they had seized upon him. Through him they were once again conjured into physical form. He was in a sense their creator, but also their slave.

For a while Margot lived with him on this new plateau of knowledge, hoping rather than believing that he had achieved his final success and that his experiments were at an end. But now the creations themselves began creating, and produced monstrosities.

At that time Margot sometimes crossed the rustic bridge into the wood, for as yet she didn't understand the nature of the elves and hoped that she might communicate with them. She saw not an elf, but the back of a tiny creature, clothed. It turned, and she saw that it had the face of a cat, much widened into a sharp-pointed oval; its mouth grinned over its needle-like fangs and its eyes were long narrow slits. It bolted at the sight of her like any wild creature, but its brief, evil glare awakened her to a new sense of horror.

Movements in the undergrowth suggested that the wood must be seething with such creatures. If ever they were emboldened enough to leave its boundaries they could cause a social nightmare. She told the Professor so in urgent language, but he seemed unreachable, and she realized that she would have to work on him with all her powers to awaken him to the danger. And then what she had long dreaded happened. Professor Bodkin was struck down. It was not a stroke, as the doctors claimed. He was obsessed. He too realized it now, too late, like a sinner who finds himself in hell. His one sound eye looked out in terror and supplication.

In the face of all this Margot remained steadfast and calm. She watched that one eye and received coded messages from it. She learned that elves distrust any mention of themselves in print and because mediaeval literature is full of magic of one kind or other she took no chances and hid all the Professor's books in a locked room. She learned that they had a way of projecting themselves on to reflecting surfaces. She learned that they would sometimes perform charitable acts, not from compassion but to please themselves, like some charitable human beings.

To keep the Professor alive she had to keep his mind alive, and to this end she read to him for hours every night, selecting the readings with extreme care. So much concentrated devotion began to affect her own nature. She became more than a dedicated bluestocking with a cerebral passion for a great scholar. The seeds of the occult implanted themselves in her system and she became initiated into some of the ways of witchcraft.

The elves recognized her as a kind of honorary sister and acknowledged her by doing their nightly rounds of chores. But there could be no coming to terms with them. Perhaps they were offended that Professor Bodkin had delved so deeply into their lore – offended in spite of the great service he had done them, for they too were capable of hating their benefactor. Margot became persuaded that they were not going to release him until a hostage could be found to take his place.

Professor Crimonesi had been a possible victim, but Margot had had reservations about him and had offered him no encouragement. Kate was different; she was young and vulnerable.

Ever since that meeting with Kate, Margot had indulged in an act of concentration that was her peculiar form of prayer. Staring into the Professor's functioning eye, she would silently ask for guidance, and when she came to conclusions of her own she took these to be spirit messages.

There was now a hint of strangeness in the air of the cottage itself, and after studying Professor Bodkin's eye as closely as if it were a piece to be moved in chess she felt impelled to go to the window and look out at Jasper doing his chores.

Jasper.

She went into the wet garden, taking a trug and hand-fork, and busied herself at his side for some minutes. Then she rose and looked him in the eye.

'Jasper,' she said, 'have you got something to tell me?'

# CHAPTER EIGHT

RELATIONSHIPS in the Crimonesi household were strained. Brenda, who was entering a stage in her life when she particularly needed to be wanted, felt neglected and overlooked because her husband and daughter, whether truly haunted or merely deluded, were *sharing* an experience from which she was shut out.

To hide her feelings she was over-bright in manner and read little books on psychology. She recited to Kate the story of a man who was put through an initiation ceremony when he joined the United States Navy. They stripped him to the waist, heated up an iron bar until it was white hot, and told him that they were going to brand him on the stomach. Then they blindfolded him. He felt the most searing, agonizing pain. He heard his flesh sizzling, he smelt it burning. What they had really done was press a piece of ice against his stomach, and thrust the hot iron into a piece of steak. But he said that the pain was the most real thing he had felt in all his life.

'All in the mind,' said Kate. 'Why are you telling me this, Mum?'

'It shows that self delusion can be very strong.'

'In some cases', said Kate, 'the self-deluding bit can be kidding yourself that you're deluded.'

Brenda smiled and pretended to go on reading, while this remark rankled with her.

Kate did not feel close to her father; she felt that their

73

relationship would never be the same again. She now knew that they were sharing a secret, and this seemed to her almost indecent. Guido must have felt the same and so, absurdly enough, they shunned the very matter which obsessed them. However, Kate finally forced herself to say, 'It's a pity we didn't keep that photo.'

'As a matter of fact I did.'

'What? The *Observer* supplement? Where?'

'Right here in my bureau drawer.'

'And you've never looked at it?'

'It's just lain there under a lot of other stuff.'

'Shall we look at it then?'

'What *are* we coming to?' muttered Guido. He still could not rid himself of his old prejudices. But he did unlock his bureau and as he removed layers of papers from the drawer, he and Kate felt as if they were reopening a grave.

Here was the *Observer* supplement intact, a little brown round the edges, but as good as new when opened at the fatal page. And there was Professor Bodkin, in a fair state of health, standing awkwardly in front of rising ground with a cream-coloured hosta to the left of his face. It was at that spot that the face of the elf had appeared. Kate fancied it lying in the drawer all those years, coming on and going out like a traffic light. However, there was no sign of it now. They looked at the photo from various angles. It looked as it must have looked in everyone else's colour supplement ten years ago. Guido found a large envelope and again submerged it in the bureau drawer.

'It wouldn't come at our bidding,' he said. 'The mystery is why it ever came at all.'

'Right, and we're not getting any further,' said Kate. 'We don't know enough.'

'You're not to go near that Croupe woman, Katie. The gardener says it's dangerous and I don't doubt he's right.'

'He's in a right muddle,' said Kate. 'No, all right, Dad,

don't worry, I'm not going to appeal to Margot Croupe, she's got some weird axe to grind. But we can't leave things as they are.'

'So what's to do? Call in an exorcist?' said Guido, with distaste.

'I was thinking of Aunt Julia. She's more on the right wavelength than we are.'

'That would be supremely ironical. I stopped believing in her magicalities long before I stopped believing in Father Christmas.'

'Yes, Dad, I know, but it might help us to be filled in on a few magicalities in the circumstances.'

'We must keep it from your mother, then.'

'No, we mustn't,' said Kate firmly.

'Katie, Aunt Julia isn't popular there, to put it mildly.'

'She'll be a sight less popular if we slink off to secret meetings with her, and so will we. Anyway, fair play, Mum has a right to be in on this.'

'Why this sudden consideration, Katie?'

'Oh, I know I've been awful to her.'

'So is this remorse or merely calculating?'

'A bit of both, perhaps. I've been brought up to calculate.' Kate hesitated. 'I suppose Adam ought to be in on it, too. *If* he's still speaking to me. I was awful to him too.'

'Why Adam?'

'Well, you see . . .'

Kate, in jealousy and pride, had left Adam out of the account she had told her parents. When Guido had assimilated this fresh piece of news he exclaimed, 'Well, then, of course he should be in on it, he's part of it. Make it up with him, Katie.'

'Dad, I walked out on him, it's not that easy–'

'Katie, just for once, do as you're told.'

'*Si Papa*,' said Kate.

*

75

Making it up with Adam was as easy as bumping a car over a ramp. Apart from his joy at getting his girlfriend back Adam was greatly relieved to rejoin the group, for he had been afraid to sleep lately for fear of dreaming and was in need of group therapy. Persuading her mother to 'chair' the meeting was also easier than Kate had expected. Brenda recognized her motives quite readily, but she was too pleased to be needed to challenge them. Miss Mandible, of course, was all too delighted to be consulted. With all the yearning of a frequenter of seances who has yet to see a ghost, she longed to share Kate's experiences, or at least to hear more of them.

Kate, having used guile on all three of them, turned her mathematical mind to the mystery itself, but it was not going to yield to her kind of reasoning. It was all too irrational. She digressed into thinking of Aunt Julia's definition of mathematics: 'A system of logic applied to numbers.' That wasn't fair; it was too dismissive. What about the creative powers that went to the making of the 'system of logic'?

'I need some of those,' she said to herself, 'because this is algebra: everything is a symbol for something else.'

The meeting couldn't be expected to solve anything but at least it brought matters into the open. The atmosphere was friendly for various personal reasons. Brenda was glad because Adam was sharing Kate's experiences; it deprived Guido of the monopoly of her feelings. Adam felt glad for the company and also because he now felt part of the family and Kate would not be able to give him up so easily. Guido was glad because Brenda must now acknowledge that he was not going mad all by himself. And Miss Mandible felt like a visiting consultant. They were all glad, in spite of the situation, because each had somehow gained from the meeting.

Brenda served coffee and for a while kept up one of those inane conversations about nothing that are the English hostess's form of preliminary sparring. When they got down to business Kate, Guido and Adam recited their stories in that order. Kate felt, curiously, that each story bore the stamp of the teller's personality. If Guido had told Adam's story, for instance, it would have sounded different even though the facts remained the same. This feeling was quite obscure and it tantalized her, because she felt that the index to the mystery somehow lay within it.

'Algebra,' she repeated to herself.

Miss Mandible said: 'Hmm. I wonder why Guido and Adam have got into this?'

'Because they have,' said Brenda rather tartly. 'Why shouldn't they?'

'The Croupe woman didn't want them to,' said Miss Mandible. 'She got rid of Guido as soon as she could and she didn't allow Adam to come near, but she welcomed you, Caterina. Perhaps Guido and Adam are like the eggs that must be broken to make an omelette.'

'I don't understand that,' said Brenda.

'I mean that they're so close to Kate that they couldn't be kept out.'

She had veered very near to the embarrassing subject of love and intimacy but, to Kate's relief, she changed the subject.

'Of course, the motives of elfin people are different from our own. We cannot explain why they do what they do. Cats are the nearest thing to them in our world. One can never quite understand the actions of cats. Or very young children. How much easier life would be for parents if their infants were reasonable. I think elves are rather like young children.'

'Or very old people,' said Kate.

'Julia,' said Brenda impatiently, 'the gardener warned

Kate about danger. I wanted to believe that the only danger lay in taking all this seriously, but who am I against the four of you? I've lost my nerve. I don't know what to believe. You seem to know something about this stuff. Tell me, what is the danger?'

'Well, there you have it,' said Miss Mandible with curious relish. 'To follow this up is dangerous, and yet to ignore it is impossible.' She glanced at Kate, darkened, and shook her head slightly. 'Yet whatever it is Miss Margot Croupe manages to live with it.'

'She's the only one who can,' said Kate quickly.

'I'm not sure about that,' said Miss Mandible. 'I suspect she's very one-sided. I'm much better balanced. I think I should make her acquaintance.'

Everyone except Kate glanced at her with carefully guarded hope, rather as the citizens of a beleaguered city might look at someone who had hinted at offering himself as a hostage. But Kate was alarmed.

'She would never agree to meet you,' she said.

'I'll get around that somehow,' said Miss Mandible.

The dead-black eyes of Margot Croupe never left Jasper's face. He was seated so that the Professor's eye fixed him as well, and felt as if he were facing both a prosecuting counsel and a hanging judge.

'But why should they visit you, Jasper?'

'They wanted to find out what was going on. It was natural enough.'

'You are saying that they found out your address and came to see you, just like that, without being invited?'

'I certainly didn't invite them.'

'What did you tell them?'

'I told them I knew nothing.'

'When the girl called here, you were sorry for her. Your exact words were, "I don't like it" and "that's a lovely kid". You are saying you didn't warn her in any way?'

'No, what could I warn her of? Anyway,' broke out Jasper belligerently, 'we've learned something, haven't we? About the boy, I mean?'

There was a very long pause indeed. 'And what did you tell him?' asked Margot at last.

'To forget it. I told him to forget it.'

Once again the ominous long silence.

'I have always kept myself to myself,' said Margot unexpectedly, 'but I've never known anyone else who does. I cannot conceive that those three are going to do so. As I've said before, it is bound to spread, and that could lead to the most impertinent interference.

'I cannot say why the father and the boy should be involved. The behaviour of the Little People is always mysterious. It has something to do with the fact that . . . they *love* the girl, I suppose.' Margot spoke the word as if it were a disease. 'I am not interested in them, except in so far as I want them out of the way.'

'And how's that going to happen?'

'Why, you're really concerned for them, aren't you, Jasper?' said Margot, raising her eyebrows. 'Well, don't imagine I'm planning to have them exterminated. They will eliminate themselves in time. But I am interested in the girl.'

'And what's to become of her?' demanded Jasper in a dry voice.

'The Little People will take her in exchange,' said Margot simply. 'Bargaining is one of their most sanctioned practices. She does not know what an honour is in store for her.' Margot closed her eyes and recited dreamily,

*Come away, O human child*
*To the waters and the wild,*
*For the world's more full of weeping than you can understand.*

'Do you know the lines? Evidently you don't. They are very beautiful, aren't they? Anyway,' she added, darkening, 'what does one cocksure little madam matter if she's replacing the greatest mind of the age? And ought she not to learn', Margot was now venomous, 'that all those charms of hers – being clever, being loved, being a "lovely kid" and flaunting her sexuality, everything she takes for granted – can be lost before she has time to reckon it?'

Jasper averted his face.

'Jasper, you seem to think that I am at fault. I am no more than a student who has researched an unusual field of knowledge. I did not make these things happen. The most I can do is help everything happen as it should.'

Jasper was staring at the floor. 'What did you mean by "eliminate themselves"?'

'I cannot say precisely. I suspect that if the Little People think them superfluous they may drive them mad. You must understand: I cannot *direct* things except in a very minor way. I do not *command* the Little People: I live on terms with them, that's all. I simply do not want any interference or misplaced concern to obstruct their will.'

'I told them I knew nothing,' said Jasper doggedly.

'That was wise of you.'

When he had gone she sat for a long while in troubled thought. Jasper was the only person in the world whom she came near to liking. She was on terms with him and long custom had made him congenial to her. But he was too kind. His misgivings in this matter were disturbing and he was likely to have them again. And if he was not wholly *for* her and her cause, he was against her, and must be considered an enemy.

Her life had been one long sacrifice. She had cut herself off from society and, in the normal intercourse of life, could hardly be said to exist. When people spoke of Professor Bodkin as a recluse they did not know the true meaning of the word. Whatever his private habits he was a household name. She was the real recluse. It had been worthwhile, up to a point, when he and she were immersed in their monumental work; it was still worthwhile, up to a point, now that she was indispensable to him – but she deserved a reward. They needed more than this precarious truce with the supernatural: they needed victory. Professor Bodkin should be in command like Merlin of old. Then she would indeed have her reward, for she would share his power, and be immortal.

Meanwhile, she must trust no one.

She sat in front of the corpse-like figure of the Professor and stared him in the eye. Sometimes it seemed that it was not he that looked back out of it, but the elfin spirit that possessed him, and that if that spirit were withdrawn he would dissolve into putrefaction. But she put this sick notion sternly from her mind like a blasphemy. She concentrated on Jasper.

The day went by, Jasper cycled home, Margot fed the Professor with liquid food through a long-stemmed feeding bottle, made him comfortable and read to him from *The Harley Lyrics* and *The Cloud of Unknowing*. She went to bed at the usual early hour and awoke at midnight to listen to the low industrious hum of her nightly helpers. It went on as usual, except that there was a slight clatter as if something had been knocked over.

She waited for the usual time to elapse and went downstairs again. She looked in at the Professor. He was asleep, his eyes closed. But the eyelid of the one sound eye glowed as if there were a light behind it.

At last she went, in a grim and suspended state, into the kitchen. She saw what had caused the clatter: on the cupboard next to the draining board a jar of salt had been tipped over. A word was traced in the spilled salt.

KILL.

# CHAPTER NINE

**B**RENDA'S TALE of the American sailor 'branded' with a piece of ice and feeling real pain had had more of an effect on Kate than she could have supposed. She found she desperately wanted to believe her mother's interpretation. For one thing, Kate, in spite of appearances to the contrary, secretly wanted to please Brenda; for another, to put everything down to imagination was very reassuring.

She therefore insisted that it was possible to deceive herself completely. Why, Mr Hermitage himself had obscurely hinted at this. So, could the sights seen and the sounds heard by herself, her father and Adam be truly imaginary? No one else had seen or heard them at the time! Aunt Julia hadn't seen the elf, and what about the creature her father claimed to have seen in the wood? Wasn't it strange that no one else had ever mentioned the wood's rare climate or its weird denizens? Wouldn't some passer-by at some time or other have happened on them? Everything pointed to the imagination which, by some strange linkage, had become common to all three of them.

She was in the china shop when she thought these thoughts, dabbing a feather duster round a shelf of cheapish objects stocked for ready sales: mice, cats, a bulbous green frog with a Disney grin and, of all things, a simpering pixie on a toadstool. The latter she found particularly offensive because, common though it was, it seemed to be mocking her efforts to be reasonable. Truth to tell, she felt out of sorts. To her kind of mind, solving a problem was a delight but to suspect that she was solving it incorrectly would make her physically uneasy. She was in this uncomfortable state when she saw that another elfin figure had joined the row on the shelf, chin in hand, smirking.

*Joined* the others? It must have been there all the time. Astonishing that she had not seen it before. She moved closer to it, and felt not just out of sorts but actually ill. She felt herself go white and her surroundings became soft and far away. She seemed to float rather than walk. The pixie's features moved. It was speaking to her, but the voice was inside her head, dreamy and echoing, lulling her away from herself . . .

But something got between her and the pixie, a sudden flash of light, caused by something in the road outside, made it turn its head and show its haggard profile. Kate looked away, and saw her own body lying on the floor of the shop.

The manageress, with the aid of two customers, helped Kate to the room behind the shop and propped her up on a chair.

'So what was all that about then?' she said. Kate thought she knew.

Someone brought her a glass of water but she didn't take it. 'Sorry,' she said, 'I passed out.'

'You did,' said the manageress, and looked at her with such significance that Kate read her thoughts.

'Oh no,' she said crossly, 'I'm not.'

'That's just as well then,' said the manageress with lingering suspicion and just a hint of disappointment. 'Well, didn't you have any breakfast this morning?'

'Yes . . . muesli . . . I can't say what happened. I looked at the elf and felt faint.'

'That little thing on a toadstool?'

'No, the other one.'

The manageress looked out into the shop. 'There isn't another one.'

Kate rubbed her eyes and held her temples. 'No, of course there isn't,' she said. 'There wouldn't be.'

'She's not quite come round,' said the customer, still hovering with the glass of water.

But the manageress, who knew what teenagers got up to, was alerted afresh. 'Do you often see imaginary things?'

'Now that's a key question,' thought Kate, but didn't say it. 'Not in working hours,' she said and stood up. 'I'm all right now. I'm sorry to be a nuisance.'

The manageress, to her credit, did not pursue the matter, but suggested Kate should sit in the back room for a while and polish some spoons. Kate, irritated at being suspected of pregnancy and drug taking, was all the more so because such suspicions were not unreasonable. But another concern soon overtook her. It was the matter of elves 'carrying off little girls'. It was not a physical kidnapping as the legends had it. They carried off one's spirit; and but for an accident of the light just now this might well have happened to hers.

She felt as if she had handed in the solution to a problem and had had it back marked 'wrong'. Her piece of reasoning had been swiftly countered. She had tried to explain everything away. However much it strained credulity, she had to reason about what was truly *there*. She would finish her day at the shop, then go to see her Aunt Julia.


'So what do I think about the Little People, as the Celtic races call them?' said Miss Mandible. 'I've always been reluctant to talk about this because my views are unfashionable, and I don't like being thought cracked, but I've always believed that inside all the myths and legends of the world there is a core of truth. It has been exaggerated and distorted over the ages, and has often been associated with fear. Have you heard of what the ancient Greeks called the "Eumenides?" Kate shook her head. 'The "Eumenides" means the "Friendly Ones". It was the name given to the savage Furies who lashed the sea into storms – a pathetic attempt to placate them. Now, what about the word "fairies"?'

'Fair ones?' suggested Kate.

'That's right. Our Celtic ancestors called them that precisely because they dreaded them. But modern man has been persuaded by science not to believe in them, and with loss of belief comes a loss of fear. It has become their fate to be sentimentalized rather than respected, relegated to the realm of make believe and children's nursery.

'I believe they are a race that has slipped out of the mainstream of evolution and has lived apart, with powers and knowledge of another kind than ours. They must have remained hidden for centuries. In the Middle Ages they were widely accepted, mixed up in a mish-mash of witches and warlocks and demons, and Professor Bodkin's mediaeval studies must have led him to them. That novel of his only brushes the surface. He must have delved much deeper; he unearthed an ancient culture.'

'And paid for it,' said Kate.

'Yes, he went too far, but that is the nature of Man. There are dangers in the jungle and the sea; they haven't stopped him from exploring. Bodkin was a pioneer. Some might think his fate worthwhile.'

'You wouldn't if you saw him,' said Kate.

'No, he's a warning to us all,' said Miss Mandible, with curious lightness, 'and the gardener was right to counsel you as he did. But he warned you too late. These things cannot be just wished away. What happened to you this morning was deeply disturbing and I'm not going to just stand by and watch.'

'What are you going to do, then?' asked Kate apprehensively.

'Caterina,' said Miss Mandible, 'I know you don't like these things said aloud, but you are very dear to me, much more than simply a surrogate niece. Now, you're bright enough, but you're impressionable, you're vulnerable and much too young to face this alone. You've asked me for help. Yes, I know by that you simply meant information. But we must be more practical than that.'

'How, practical?'

'I shall make enquiries,' said Miss Mandible equably. 'No, don't ask me how; I don't know yet. But I'm just the person for the job. I have the advantage of your father's scientific training, balanced by a quite serious belief in the learning of Professor Bodkin. Miss Margot Croupe may have reason to be afraid of me.'

'I'm afraid *for* you,' said Kate miserably. 'I shouldn't have dragged you into this.'

'Dragged is a bit strong,' said Miss Mandible, smiling. 'You might even say I gatecrashed.'

'Oh isn't it difficult to sort out people's actions from their motives,' said Kate vexedly.

'Not to mention the motives of elves,' said Miss Mandible.

'And you're determined to find out what they are?'

'Certainly I shall make enquiries.'

'Let me enquire with you, then.'

'On no account, Caterina. You'd spoil everything.'

'It's Julia, for you,' said Brenda.

'She wants my cooperation,' said Guido, returning from the phone.

'In what way?'

'She wants me to get in touch with the gardener, Hermitage.'

'So much for her "leave it all to me" stance,' said Brenda bitterly.

'It's quite reasonable. Hermitage has met me and he knows I'm Kate's father. I've got a right to question him. Julia's a stranger to him; he'd not agree to meet her.'

'He didn't tell me much,' said Kate.

'It's like a police enquiry, Katie. Any bit of information will help. I think Aunt Julia wants to build up a picture of Margot Croupe and her ways. It's our only way in.'

'I wish I knew what she's trying to achieve,' said Brenda.

'Brenda, it's plain commonsense –'

'Oh, I know. You needn't go into details, I think I'm just about intelligent enough to get the general idea. But I don't see things in black and white like you, Guido. I'd just like to know what Julia's after.'

'Why this attack on Julia?'

'I am not *attacking* her.'

'But what are your objections?'

'I can't say as yet.'

'I must say that makes everything radiantly clear.'

Kate was silent and unhappy, sympathizing with them both.

# CHAPTER TEN

'WELL?' ASKED MISS MANDIBLE.

'That gardener chap has a rather touching respect for learning,' replied Guido. 'He was quite deferential to me. Called me sir. He told me quite a lot.'

'Yes?'

'As we know, that wood has some gruesome creatures in it. He and the Croupe woman tend that garden scrupulously to keep them at bay – it seems they suffer from a form of agoraphobia.'

'Creatures of the dark,' said Miss Mandible, with peculiar relish. 'What else did he tell you?'

'Margot Croupe has some kind of telepathic communication with Professor Bodkin. He's as helpless as a newborn babe, but Hermitage thinks she gets her orders from him. Of course he has no idea how. He also believes that some kind of murky ritual goes on at midnight.'

'Midnight,' mused Miss Mandible. 'The witching hour. How extremely interesting.'

'Julia, we're not just preparing a paper on all this.'

'No indeed. Now go over everything he told you in minutest detail, Guido. Omit nothing.'

After a dismal July, said to be the wettest since records began, the weather turned to a heatwave. Jasper Hermitage was not the sort of gardener to work stripped to the waist and invariably wore a layer or two. By the end of the day he must have sweated away pounds. As he fetched his bicycle and stood by it for a moment, mopping his brow, Margot Croupe said to him, 'Jasper, why don't you leave your coat behind? It will be terribly hot cycling home in it.'

A suggestion from Margot was really an order, and with dark misgivings he hung up his coat in the porch. It was of blue serge, shiny with wear, and had at one time been part of a suit.

Margot went through the evening's routine with such formality that she might have been a piece moving on a chess board, but with one extra move. Returning John Gower's *Confessio Amantis* to the upstairs room, she fetched some papers from a drawer at the bottom of a bookcase and pored over them. Finally, nodding to herself, resolved, she fetched Jasper's coat from the porch. Its lining, she noted with satisfaction, was stained with sweat. From it she managed to pull out a long thread, which she carried out to the garden, replacing the coat in the porch as she went. She took a pair of long-handled shears from the shed and went to the very end of the garden, working herself along behind the cupressus trees to face the water. A narrow strip of tufty grass led down to the lake, with a few bits of prickly sow-thistle growing in it. She leaned as far as she could over the wire fence, snipped off a sprig of this and, holding it gingerly between the blades of the shears, brought it in. She took the thread from Jasper's coat and wound it round the thistle, tying it tight. She threw the thistle into the water.

She returned to the house, quite composed, but saddened, for she was in fact fond of Jasper.

Miss Mandible spent the evening washing and rearranging her figurines. They were to her as dolls are to young children, but she hadn't the child's gift of make-believe and their fixed posturing finally repelled her. Guido's words about 'some murky ritual at midnight' ran through her head, with their implication of enchanted life. She visualized parades and ceremonial dances, with perhaps some fetish of a sacrifice, with an overture of elfin piping. Perhaps the animal-headed creatures from the wood would encircle it, filling the darkness with the glittering points of their eyes. These were frightening thoughts, but they fascinated her, and her longing to be involved was irresistible.

She calculated over and over again how long it would take her to drive to Dovecot Lane, for to arrive at exactly the right moment seemed of absolute importance. At some twenty minutes to midnight she went out to her car, patted herself all over with unusual thoroughness to make sure that she had her house-keys, driving licence and various other necessities about her, and set off. As she drove she dwelt on unpleasant and somewhat unlikely mishaps, like having an accident or witnessing a crime, which would delay her arrival, but she reached Dovecot Lane punctually, parked her car not far from the entrance and began making the rest of the way on foot.

The ground was new to her, and as she crept along, using a small hand torch at intervals, she tensed herself to face whatever might show up in its circle of light. But she passed the rustic bridge and came to Professor Bodkin's cottage without seeing anything out of the ordinary, nor hearing anything other than some slight rustlings of nature.

A dark shape by the gate made her catch her breath, but the flick of her torch showed it to be no more than a box for the post. The cottage was dark and still. Had she come in vain? Was she in for a repetition of her experience in Kate's home? The thought made her quite sick with disappointment. Still she lingered, pathetically refusing to accept this vacancy. And then everything changed. The air became 'live' like an open telephone line. She knew that there was movement: in the garden, up to the house, into the house.

It was silent but all-pervading. It thrilled and yet menaced her, and she had to steel herself to stand still, as one does on a railway platform when an express thunders by. But she saw nothing.

It was terrible to be present at this happening and yet not to witness it. A supreme experience was passing her by, and she envied Kate, she bitterly envied Kate, the little sceptic who was the privileged one.

As she waited it seemed to her that the invaders left the cottage and again moved across the garden, but they were no longer urgent with purpose and their going was very gentle. Still she stood there, with the obstinacy that will not admit failure. She stood there for a full fifteen minutes. To return to her car would be a wretched anticlimax. Like a moth lured by a flame she opened the gate and groped her way, step by step, along the parterre. Her eyes were accustomed to the dark now, and she manoeuvred the sundial and reached the front door, which of course was shut. At last she realized the absurd futility of what she was doing and turned away. As she did so, she heard a door close somewhere at the side of the house. As far as it was possible in the dark, she hurried, for her presence here was indefensible. But now the front door opened, light poured out, and Margot Croupe, in a dressing-gown, came out onto the porch.

Miss Mandible said, 'I am Kate Crimonesi's godmother.'

Which was untrue but the best she could do. She awaited annihilation. But Margot simply replied, coldly and calmly, 'Just what do you hope to achieve?'

Miss Mandible's combative spirit came to her aid. She said, 'I hoped to see your midnight visitors.'

Margot, with complete composure, said, 'And did you?'

'I—'

'Evidently you did not.'

Miss Mandible expected Margot to call the police. But

Margot seemed amazingly incurious about the sheer impudence of this intrusion. She said indifferently, 'Where did you get the idea that I have midnight visitors?'

'Isn't it traditional?'

'Is it? That seems a very weak excuse for coming here at this time of night and putting yourself at my mercy . . . and theirs.'

Fear made Miss Mandible angry. 'Miss Croupe,' she said, 'don't take advantage of me. You must know why I'd go to such lengths. Kate is very dear to me and I want her set free, you know from what. If I can achieve that, I don't care what happens to me.'

This noble speech was, of course, not quite genuine. Margot almost certainly saw through it. She actually laughed, perhaps for the first time in years.

'I'm still at a loss to know your intentions,' she said. 'However, we can't discuss it here. You'd better come in.'

Miss Mandible, who had been wrong-footed throughout these exchanges, could only say, formally, 'You're very kind.'

'No,' said Margot, 'the truth is, since you've come so far, I can't let you go.'

# CHAPTER ELEVEN

MISS MANDIBLE was conducted to the kitchen, given a rush-seated chair and offered coffee. She did not like Margot Croupe, but she recognized that she was being let off lightly and explained herself apologetically. She cleared up the little inaccuracy about being a godmother, and described her relationship with Guido and Kate. She outlined their experiences, stressing how they had sought her advice. As if to ingratiate herself with Margot, she emphasized how seriously she took the Little People, and repeated briefly what she had said about them to Kate. Margot's face was like that of an austere examiner at an oral.

'For a layperson', she remarked at last, 'you are remarkably well informed. Let us get one thing perfectly clear, however. You are not acting on Kate's behalf. You are acting on your own behalf.'

This hit home. 'Does that matter?' asked Miss Mandible.

'Yes, very much. The Little People are never taken in. They understand your motives which – please don't think me impertinent, Miss Mandible – are not unlike those of women who steal babies from prams.'

Miss Mandible flushed a heavy red.

'A false comparison, Miss Croupe. Babies in prams do not invite people to steal them. The elves deliberately lure people. If I'm acting on my own behalf, it's because I can't help myself.'

'That is a very old belief, but it's a mistake,' said Margot.

'People are lured by their own wishes.'

'That's simply not true. Kate saw the elf at the age of eight. It happened out of the blue. You're telling me she wished it?'

'I can't say how it is with her,' said Margot, 'but I know that we wish at different levels of our minds. Our conscious wishes often turn out to be the very last things we really wanted, but there are deeper wishes that are never false. They may have painful consequences, but they are what we truly desire, and that must be the case with that young girl.'

'She's in danger,' said Miss Mandible angrily. 'You must know what danger. Do you deny that you are encouraging it? Is that your deep wish? Isn't it a wicked one?'

'I can only play my part.'

Miss Mandible stared at the pale, set face in dismay. She was sure that Margot had rare, deep knowledge, and that such knowledge without morality was deadly; but to lose her temper would serve nothing.

'"Lured by our own wishes",' she said. 'Are you saying that elves exist only in human minds?'

'That's both true and untrue.'

Margot became didactic.

'Man thinks of nothing original. He gives names to things, or he assembles to his advantage what is already there. For instance, he has invented television, but the components that make up a television set must have existed since time began. The spirit world to which elves belong existed long before Man, but Man's mind has defined them, given them a local habitation and a name, as Shakespeare said. Professor Bodkin's research took him right back into that ancient, naming time. He discovered and practised rituals that had lain untouched for centuries. He revived parts of the mind, his own mind, which had all but atrophied. By the sheer power of thought he brought the elfin world back into existence.

'The old magicians had this same power, but they handled it more easily, because the climate of ideas in their time was so much more favourable than it is now. Their understanding of the elfin world outside our own was so deep that they actually brought the Little People on to this planet as separate and living beings. They gave birth to them, as it were. It was wonderful, although not more wonderful than our modern miracles: radar, the computer, nuclear power. Modern people take these things for granted, while elves are dismissed as childish nonsense. Professor Bodkin had to work in this climate, and at the peak of his marvellous achievement, he collapsed under the strain.

'He was no longer able to control his creation, and what is created never stays still. By maintaining a strict routine I have kept the elves in check, and by constant devotion to Professor Bodkin I have kept his own spirit alive. But the genie was out of the bottle. The elves multiplied and produced their own horrible side issues. And now it has become apparent that for all my efforts I have not been able to prevent them from appearing to the outside world. Professor Bodkin must be freed. But I don't know it all. I can only play my part.'

'Why have you told me all this?'

Margot smiled faintly. 'Foolish of me.' She rose. 'Now you can go.'

'I suppose I wasn't worth keeping after all,' said Miss Mandible dourly.

'Count yourself fortunate,' said Margot. 'Goodnight, Miss Mandible. I hope there will be no repercussions.'

'What kind of repercussions?'

'There's no knowing,' said Margot. 'You didn't see them, Miss Mandible, but be sure they saw you.'

Miss Mandible trudged back to her car feeling defeated. She inserted her key in the ignition and turned it. Nothing happened. She tried several times. Nothing happened.

'This is all I need,' she muttered.

She walked to the end of Dovecot Lane and looked for a phone box. By good fortune there was one just opposite. She rang the AA. The AA man turned the key and the engine obligingly started and settled into a good-tempered hum.

'You must think I'm foolish,' said Miss Mandible.

'That's all right,' said the AA man. Lonely old women panicked easily, especially at this time of night.

'I wonder . . .' said Miss Mandible awkwardly, 'I wonder if you would mind seeing me home?'

'Well, where's home? . . . Oh, no distance. Sure, I'll be right behind you.'

He followed her into Roydene Crescent and watched her leave her car.

'All right now?'

'Thank you very much indeed.'

Thank Heavens, she was home.

Her door was the right-hand one of a pair in the porch. She turned her house-key in the lock. The door would not open.

She removed the key, thrust it in again, twisted it, shook it. Her efforts made the knocker flap about but the door would not open. She pounded it with her fists and kicked it. She leaned against the wall, panting. She renewed her assault. The door of number 23 opened and her neighbour, in a dressing-gown, looked out apprehensively.

'What's wrong, Julia?'

'It's ridiculous, but –'

'Let me try.' He took the key. His wife appeared in the doorway. They were a youngish couple, decent.

'Might just need a drop of oil,' he said.

But the front door opened sweetly.

'There you are!'

'I'm terribly sorry to have disturbed you.'

'No problem!'

Miss Mandible succeeded in putting herself to bed, moving very cautiously. What had happened had been no coincidence. It had been very annoying, but what really upset her was that it had been so trivial. These were the sorts of tricks played by Puck on milkmaids.

'All I'm fit for, I suppose,' she said, and felt unwanted and old.

# CHAPTER TWELVE

THE NEXT MORNING Miss Mandible's neighbour asked her in for coffee. Miss Mandible, who now dreaded leaving her maisonette for fear of being unable to reopen the front door, asked her in instead but since she could not get the electric kettle to work the neighbour took over and made the coffee for her.

'There's something wrong,' said the neighbour. 'She can't do simple things. She couldn't open the biscuit tin.'

'Old age,' said her husband.

'She's not that old.'

'Well, *we* can't do much about it. Hasn't she got any relations?'

'Well, we have found out the address of those people who call on her. I'm going to give them a ring.'

It was Sunday and immediately after the call Kate went with her mother to Roydene Crescent. Brenda was being very kind to Miss Mandible in her new helplessness. It was quite inconsistent. She could perform normally for a period of time, and then, when she all but thought herself released, some fresh silliness would thwart her: she would fail to fit a plug in its socket; a cup would refuse to leave its hook on the dresser. These annoyances strained her nerves to the limit. Brenda was being most forbearing, which annoyed Miss Mandible even more, but in all fairness it is hard to see how Brenda could have behaved better.

The worst of it was that Miss Mandible was restrained

by dread from making any positive move – almost, indeed, from moving at all. She could, however, speak freely, and, to dispel any doubts that she was affected by age, related in detail all that Margot had told her in sharp and caustic tones. 'According to that woman', she said, 'the elves are mental concepts made physical. Of course, so are mathematical formulae, so are poems. But at least they have to be written down by human hand. The elves sprang straight from the Professor's head, like –'

'Like the goddess Athena from the head of Zeus?' supplemented Brenda, and raised one eyebrow at Kate. 'Oh yes dear, I do know one or two things that you don't. I can't help feeling, Julia, that if the elves are products of thought they can be overcome by thought.'

'Yes,' said Miss Mandible, 'if anyone has a brain like Professor Bodkin and can devote a lifetime to it.'

'No,' said Kate.

'Well well, the voice of authority,' said Miss Mandible. 'What then, Caterina?'

'Something else,' said Kate. 'I mean it's not just a matter of brains and study. You have to *feel* with them, sort of.'

'To meddle with feelings', said Miss Mandible, 'can be very distressing.'

'You're quite involved enough already, Kate,' said Brenda. 'You've seen what involvement does.'

'She means me,' said Miss Mandible.

'No, no,' said Brenda hastily. 'I meant everyone.'

'Presumably that includes me,' said Miss Mandible.

Kate was sorry for her mother, patiently enduring snubs, but Brenda antagonized her too. She felt, curiously, that if their positions were reversed, she would take exactly the same line as her mother, but this did not endear Brenda to her, quite the reverse; it grated on her nerves.

She said to Adam later, 'I don't know, but I think I'm closer to Mum than to Dad in some ways.'

'This is something new,' said Adam. 'I thought you and your dad were so close you were practically overlapping.'

'Yes, we are, but he loves me like he loves astronomy or the Quantum Theory. Like you love music. I think Mum hates me a lot of the time, but there's more red blood in it. Dad's a funny Italian. They're supposed to be all palpitating with emotion but he's always been the opposite. And of course I've been brought up to be the same. And you know what? It's got something to do with why I saw the elf. Yes, really. I can't possibly say why, but it has, something in my make-up put me on its wavelength.'

'And took some others along with you,' said Adam.

'Adam, I'm really sorry about that. I know I bitch about your music sometimes, but I really am sorry.'

'I'm learning to live with it. No more dreams. I had that horrendous one after we'd had a quarrel,' said Adam.

He sounded heroic and piteous, for he was making a little capital out of it at Kate's expense. She could forgive him as much, but she was struck by how devious, how loaded with ulterior motive, is so much of what we say. The elves did not have a monopoly of mischief. But the lesson was that human minds had given birth to them.

'Good if you're coming to terms with it,' she ventured.

'It was after you said they'd given me something they didn't mean me to have,' said Adam.

'Was it, Adam?' said Kate eagerly. 'I think that's very important.'

'Well, maybe. I don't know how I'm supposed to use it. Some sort of Pied Piper act? Am I going to troop them all behind me and drown them in the lake?'

'Time will tell, I suppose.'

'Let's hope so. I just know I dare not play that tune just yet. It'd be like firing a gun too soon.'

*

'Jasper,' said Margot Croupe, 'there are weeds growing in the grassy slope behind the fence.'

'Well, there would be.'

'I'd feel happier if they were dug up.'

'I might as well weed the whole lane.'

'But these are so near.'

'Be tricky getting to them.'

'Yes, take care.'

He looked at her with sullen resignation and slouched off. He knew that she was not really concerned with the weeds beyond the fence and she knew that he knew. There was a dark, unspoken understanding between them.

Yet in fact she had made this last unreasonable demand out of compassion. She had not expected that the spell would have such lingering effects. She wanted his death swift and sudden. The present sight of him shocked her. In a very short time he had lost an alarming amount of weight. His skin seemed to be two sizes too big for him. His throat sagged in bloodhound folds. He had a scholarly face, probably on account of his dumb worship of scholarship, but it was drawn and hollow-cheeked and his eyes were faded. His whole appearance suggested a hunted quarry ready to submit. It truly hurt her to see him looking so ill, because she was fond of him.

She too was not feeling well, although her pallid looks did not betray it. She was beginning to doubt herself. She knew that Miss Mandible was having just the right amount of trouble; she had made sure of that by planting it in her mind when she said, 'I hope there will be no reper-cussions...' and, secretly trailing her back to her car, she had been satisfied to see that the trouble had begun. But otherwise things were not working out quite as they should. Jasper, she was sure, was parleying further with the Crimonesis. Instinct told her that neither Professor Crimonesi nor young Adam Longfellow were declining as they ought to be. The messages of elves, whether transmitted through Professor Bodkin's eye or written in salt, were cryptic. Margot was a devout student but she was not the master, and for all her care she might not always get them right. This, if the truth were known, rankled with her in her heart of hearts, although her devotion to the Professor was absolute.

Had she told Miss Mandible too much? What else could she do to quench her compulsive curiosity but satisfy it and then render her helpless? It might still have been a mistake. It threw doubt on all she did. *Kill?* Why? To prevent Jasper from giving any more away? That was not working, and anyway she was now as guilty as he. Kill? How? If it were simply by draining his life away she might be killing herself as well, for this slow attrition was terrible to watch.

She went into the garden and looked about for him. He was not to be seen. It was very quiet. She began to walk slowly through the garden. Jasper reappeared with a trug full of weeds and put them on the bonfire.

She was very disappointed and very relieved.

That night, when she went to her room, she did not go to bed, but sat in an armchair and thought. The situation needed Kate Crimonesi, needed her total involvement, needed her *now*. There had been moments of near victory already, but they had slipped away. It was like playing a big fish that must be reeled in before it gets beyond control. There must be no more waiting.

When midnight came and the hum of activity began below, Margot crept out on to the landing and, trembling all over, went downstairs and into the kitchen. Anticipation made her feel faint, for in all her years of study she had never seen an elf face to face. She expected to see them now, the terrible Little People, as clearly as she had seen their progeny in the wood. She expected an innumerable swarm with the ceaseless activity of bees. But they were too quick for her eyes to focus on them. Now and again she thought she saw a tiny green-clad figure, but it was gone before she could be certain. And yet she knew that the air was full of them. The hum that she was accustomed to hearing in her bedroom had become a whine so thin and high that it was hardly audible. She felt it in her head, shrill with anger, and knew that she had done what ancient legend denounced as unforgivable: she had spied on them, she had broken the code.

Nevertheless Margot braced herself with all the defiance of a fallen angel. Her mouth and throat were too dry for speech, but she spoke in her head as if she were praying.

*I have kept faith with you all these years. Help me.*

The whine ceased, or rather, it spun off into so high a pitch that it was lost; it seemed to suck all life from the air and left a vacuum behind. Margot slipped into unconsciousness and when she came to on the kitchen floor a few minutes later there was nothing left in the night air but emptiness and a sense of loss.

She picked herself up as one might after a desperate combat, not knowing if it were lost or won but glad it was over. She went to the Professor. He was awake, his one sound eye phosphorescent in the dark. She switched on a side-light, keeping him in shadow, and examined his face. For the first time since his paralytic fit, his lips moved, his lower jaw quivered. She knelt by him, straining for any syllable. But the spasm passed and his face again became cold and dead.

She tended him and went back to her room, exhausted, with hardly the energy to undress. She awoke unusually late and when she sat before her mirror to put up her dull black hair she saw that it was no longer black. It was white, a dead white, the colour of death.

\*

'What did you mean by algebra?' asked Guido.

Kate found this difficult. In her earlier years at school she would often get her work back with *Working must be shown* on it in urgent red ink. Like many people who are very good at mathematics, she could usually see the answer to a problem before she knew how she had reached it. Explanation was a bore. 'Can't you *see* it is?' her brain would protest.

'Well,' she said, 'algebra uses symbols, doesn't it?'

'It does indeed,' said Guido patiently.

'And Margot Croupe told Aunt Julia that elves are the product of the human mind?'

'Not exactly,' said Guido judicially. 'I understand her to say that the human mind *defines* them, rather.'

'But that's it,' said Kate eagerly. 'There's no such thing as *the* human mind. There are only individual minds, yours and mine and Margot's and so on. And when it comes to an unknown quantity like elves, each mind will interpret it differently.'

'So that's where the algebra comes in? We put our own values on these phenomena?'

'Yes. We decide what they're *for*. What they actually *want*.'

'And we can all be different but equally right?'

'Equally wrong, rather.'

Guido looked with adoration at his daughter. The way to his heart was through his brain. 'You've got something of the mystic in you, Katie *mia*,' he said. 'It's bad mathematics.'

'It's entirely logical.'

'I don't doubt the Croupe woman is sure she's right.'

'That's her opinion.'

'And you've got yours.'

'Yes,' said Kate, 'but my opinion is what I believe to be the truth.'

They discussed the subject for some time and, distressing though it was, they were happier in this intellectual exchange than they had been for weeks. But when the glow of mutual tenderness had faded, Kate said to herself, 'Saying *because* doesn't get me far,' and felt as downcast as she had been happy.

She awoke that night well after midnight with a strange feeling of unrest and a high, thin, continuous whining sound in her ears. Her instinct told her that this was some echo from the cottage: a tide was loosed, chaos had come. Then all went quiet, and the quiet was more ominous than the disturbance. A little later she became aware, in the same way that one will discern the ticking of a clock by listening for it, that a presence of some kind was at hand.

When she had first seen the elf's reflection in her window she had dreaded that its physical body was in her room. It had not been there, of course. This was.

## CHAPTER THIRTEEN

KATE DID NOT DARE to move, even to bury herself under the bedclothes. She wished she could cross herself or chant some piece of scripture, anything at all to ward off whatever incubus was about to descend upon her.

Moving only her eyes, she saw it by the left-hand wall, in the dark patch above her bookcase; its shoulders hunched and angular, its hands like claws. It was lit by some faint glow of its own, and as she eyed it, as nervously as if it had been a bedside cobra, it seemed to her that it was not an image, not another projection, but solid, the thing itself; and if it touched her she would die of disgust.

She sat up, on guard, and saw that now there was not one visitor, there were two. The wraith of Professor Bodkin was by the bookcase. He stood as he had done in the picture, a mildly doddering figure, but his face was frightful, the old mouth twitching, the one sound eye frenzied. His head was on a level with the hideous little manikin and the two of them merged together and glided apart like shadows on a wall.

She saw him only for seconds. The old man's visage dissolved and the elf turned on its perch on the bookcase and became sweet-faced. The transformation was incredible: it had become a sentimental fib again, a picture-card elf. Now it spoke, in a tiny, pretty voice that lisped inside her head.

'Come away . . .'

It was so beguiling, its charm brought such a warm flow of relief after the recent horror, that she almost willed herself to leave her body and drift wherever he led her. Wasn't our loathsome world well lost for the dreamworld of fairyland?

There was also a most subtle appeal to self-sacrifice, and no appeal is stronger. Wasn't it a kind of duty, to give herself in exchange for the captured spirit of that pitiful old man, like a sacrificial maiden of legend?

But she looked at it again in the dark, perching there in its gentle, alluring glow, and she saw treachery in the diamond-bright dots of its eyes. Our world might be loathsome, but it had conceived its own ideas of justice. For this creature fair exchange would have no meaning. She cried out in sudden rage:

'*Vai via! Via! Non mi vincera nai! Via, Via!*'

In the same moment she tugged the light cord above her bed, and in the pop of a bubble the elf was gone, leaving her in doubt as to whether he had really been solid after all.

She seemed to have won that round, and was astonished at the suddenness of the victory. It was as if all resistance had relaxed, leaving her clutching at nothing. Her mind, in this vacuum, made one of its quantum leaps. Why had Professor Bodkin made this second, pitiable spirit visit? Certainly not to entice Kate to his own predicament. He had been looking in desperation for any means of breaking free. Free from elfin bondage, of course. But from another bondage too.

Margot, reported by Aunt Julia, had said that our very deepest wishes were often buried under what we imagined we wished. Margot, like so many earnest preachers before her, did not consider this to apply to her. Kate's guess, in short, was that Margot had not truly wished to prevent the spell from enslaving Professor Bodkin; she had secretly wanted it.

But what did that conclusion lead to? There was no proof of it anyway. *Working must be shown*, the red ink injunction had said. Kate could not do that. She had made a leap in the dark. She could not commit her conclusion to paper, nor explain it in a court of law, but she had the conviction of the religious convert and was resolute in her dogma. She was mysteriously thrilled, as if she had discovered a new dimension.

Now she thought of her father and Adam, presumably lying asleep, and she felt quite aggrieved that they should be so while she had been through such an ordeal. But perhaps the linkage was working and they were tormented by dreams. She longed to question them there and then, but her own house was silent, and ringing Adam at this hour would cause such a disruption at his lodgings that her respect for convention prevailed.

Guido was neither asleep nor dreaming. He was awake in that bleak time of the night, the small hours, when self-doubt troubles us most. In a world of war, famine and global ruin it was ignominious to be preoccupied with elves; but his self-respect was undermined in other ways. He had always felt himself to be the master of his life: a brilliant and charismatic lecturer, a good and just husband and father, he had been in all ways unanswerably *right*. But now he was no longer in command. He was no longer his daughter's mentor – their roles were reversed: Kate was now instructing him, and on her own terms. He was abdicating, she ruled. He was exceedingly proud of her, he had waited with glowing confidence for her to reach adult status, but he hadn't been prepared for the change.

Not through any skill of his would the haunting be stopped. If ever it were, he would be no more than a spectator to it.

*

111

Adam, meanwhile, was neither asleep nor dreaming, but obsessed with the elfin tune, which was more insistent than ever before. It kept changing its rhythm: sometimes it went diddy-*dah*, diddy-*dah*, and then it would go *dah*-diddy, *dah*-diddy. He found himself fitting words to it: *come* away, *come* away, or alternatively come-a-*way*, come-a-*way*; and this shifting rhythmic process went on and on, fretting and teasing him. Something had happened. There was a new disturbance in the wood. Was he really being summoned to play the Pied Piper role? He would have none of the Pied Piper's guarantees. He saw himself condemned to conduct those animal-headed creatures of his dream, which were real enough if Guido was to be believed; and there would be no River Weser to drown them in.

Miss Mandible was also awake. Her latest humiliation was that she had been unable to get into bed. The nights being warm, she had a sheet and one thin blanket on it, but she could not get herself between the sheet and the undersheet and, after much furious ruffling, had to settle for lying under the blanket, with the top sheet underneath her. The first insulting symptoms of old age, she thought, but that was not true; she was vigorous and strong and her brain was clear. She lay awake in an exceedingly bad temper, thinking over the petty nuisances of the day, until she threw off the blanket and went to the kitchen to make a cup of tea.

Something, she indistinctly felt, was in the air, something new, a kind of mental pins and needles, but she had had enough of these unseen manifestations and shuffled about her kitchen in a mood to kick any elf that dared to show itself. She boiled the water, put the tea in the pot and the milk in the cup without mishap, but when she came to add sugar (she allowed herself half a teaspoonful) she found that she was pouring salt instead.

She was about to hurl the salt cellar at the wall when she was prevented by the softest, silkiest touch on her wrist. At this she flushed, her mouth went dry and her heart thundered. She was weak with fear and tremulous with elation.

*Salt.* It played quite a part in legendary spells. Sure that her hand was being guided, she poured the contents of the salt cellar on to her mica-topped kitchen table and smoothed the grains with her hand. They swirled and tingled, or so she thought, as if they were iron filings moved by a magnet from below. She waited for a revelation: a message traced in the salt, or for its particles to form themselves into a face. Nothing happened.

Now that, one would suppose, was the overwhelmingly likely outcome of such an experiment. Ah, but nothing happened *on purpose*. The touch on her wrist had been real, the tingle under her hand had been real and this refusal of the salt to move had not been the natural behaviour of an inanimate object. It denoted elfin malice refusing to respond. Miss Mandible had asked too much. She was rejected again.

She felt as she had in her youth when, at a dance, a young man would walk invitingly up to her and then pass her by, having raised her hopes only to dash them. She gave up the idea of tea and went back to her bedroom. She got between the sheets without difficulty and, as if she were drugged, fell asleep at once. In the morning she did everything very carefully for fear of incurring some further bother, but it wasn't necessary. She was rejected, the spell was lifted.

'She's a little old lady,' muttered Jasper.

In the ten years that he had known Margot she had not noticeably aged. She was tall for a woman and unbending, as though she had been trained to wear a backboard like an early Victorian schoolgirl and had never removed it. She had a fixity of manner, scholarly and austere, so that it was hard to believe that she had ever been young or would grow any older. She still stood straight, her black eyes still stared levelly, but she now had a crumpled look as though her flesh were collapsing through her skeleton; her white hair made her face look even more pallid and emphasized its lines. She looked terminally tired. Jasper, who could hardly drag himself about, felt profoundly guilty. He was in awe of Margot. She was to him a superior being and it shocked him that to bring about his end she had to ruin herself.

He made no comment on her pitiful appearance but got on with his job, trimming and cutting and hoeing the soil, but the old urgency had gone out of it. Once or twice he went to the boundary fence and stared across the water at the wood as if daring its horde, but the very wood seemed dead. All that day Jasper experienced an aimlessness so dreadful that he might almost have died and been wandering about the garden as a ghost. At midday he did not join Margot for lunch as usual, but munched his sandwiches outdoors and drank his tea from the thermos. She did not question this; it seemed right.

Margot did not help him in the garden. She saw to the Professor's needs, was left with time on her hands, and moved indecisively about the house as if uncertain whether to do the housework or not. After a while she sat down before the Professor and stared at his eye in bitter reproach.

That evening she fed him and tended him as scrupulously as ever but for the first time since his collapse she did not read to him. She spent the evening in another room, bowed in thought. She went to bed at her usual early hour and lay awake until midnight.

She listened. She would have welcomed the usual hum of activity so much that it would have restored her strength, but she heard nothing, and the silence seemed full of threat.

After a while she got up and dressed. She made her way with a hand torch to the boundary fence, weaving her way behind the cupressus trees, which hemmed her in, making a quick retreat impossible. Her torch made the edges of ripples glisten in the water, and when she turned its long narrow wand of light on the wood it picked out glittering pinpoints, a spangled spread of them, throughout the range of the trees.

She whispered, 'I do not want him tortured like this.'

A gust of wind ruffled the leaves and slapped the water against the bank, and the pinpoints formed new constellations.

She cried aloud, 'I command you to end it! I command you! End it, end it!'

With her hair blown about the white mask of her face she looked the picture of a demented witch. The wood gave back a faint echo to her shout. There was no other response. Margot crumpled, squirmed her way past the cupressus trees, and dragged herself back to the house.

# CHAPTER FOURTEEN

KATE DID NOT ASK her father whether or not he had passed a peaceful night. She suspected that some change had taken place, for better or worse, but she now wanted to keep this to herself. To probe too early would spoil things, like opening a darkroom before a photograph was fully developed. She did however tentatively ask her mother if Dad was all right.

'As well as can be expected,' said Brenda. 'What a pity that you ever mentioned what you saw in that picture. Oh, I'm not blaming you, but it was a pity, because otherwise you would have thought it was meant to be there and he would never have heard of it, and none of this would have happened.'

'I've thought about it ever since, on and off,' said Kate. 'But not the elf, the quarrel.'

'Oh, some quarrel!' said Brenda. 'Do you realize what some kids have to put up with?'

'It just stuck with me, that's all.'

'No doubt because you've been so spoilt,' said Brenda. 'Why did you ask about Dad?'

Kate said something noncommittal and set off for work, but once clear of her road she phoned the china shop, pretended a bilious attack, and took herself with strange anticipation to Aunt Julia's.

'If you have come to wash the dishes or assist me to the loo,' said Miss Mandible acidly, 'you need not have bothered. The *status quo* is restored.'

'What's that?'

'Your ignorance is a barrier to normal conversation. I mean the annoyances have ceased.'

'Oh! Oh well, that's great . . .'

'Quite so. You need not worry about me. Just understand that I'm of no importance.'

'Oh yes you are, Auntie. You of all people.'

'Oh?'

'Yes. I think you hold the key to it all.'

'Sit down, Caterina.' Miss Mandible left the room to make the invariable coffee, and when she returned her manner had noticeably softened.

'I'm surprised that you should say this,' she said, 'because my interference has been treated with contempt, both by the Croupe woman and our little friends.' She waited for the coffee to brew in the cafetière, ceremonially depressed the plunger, and poured. Then with some hesitation she told Kate what had happened in the night. 'You see?' she said. 'I was let off with a caution, as it were. I simply don't count.'

'I should look on the bright side,' said Kate, who was recovering her nerve. 'It doesn't matter if the elves rate you or not. I rate you very highly.'

'Why, Caterina?'

'Because you know so much about Dad.'

'Well?'

'Because I don't believe I wished the elf on him. I believe he wished it on me.'

'Good heavens, child, how do you make that out?'

'Tell me about reading him fairy stories when he was little.'

'I've told you already. He really loved them, but he wouldn't let himself. I had to stop reading them, because he would end up shouting that they were impossible and would fly into a tantrum.'

118

'What about going to church?'

'There again, he wouldn't let himself enjoy it. They're very impressive, you know, those great Italian services with the priests all dressed up. I'm afraid my scepticism infected him. Anyway he rebelled against it.'

'Against his parents,' said Kate.

'Ah, that's a good bit of amateur psychology, Caterina, but where is this leading to?'

'Dad is an Italian who tries to be as un-Italian as possible. He's an Italian father who loves his Italian daughter – it's always choked me even to say that, but I've got to, it's a practical fact – and he unconsciously wished on me what he himself had missed out on as a child. Of course he always treated me as a miniature intellectual adult, and I played back to him. Kids will play any role when they know what's wanted of them, but deep down, in those buried wishes that old Margot told you about, he wanted me to believe in fairies.'

'My dear Caterina, this is somewhat far-fetched!'

'Well, of course it is, but it's the Sherlock Holmes thing you mentioned, whatever-remains-however-improbable-must-be-the-truth. I'm not saying that Dad actually said to himself, "I want her to see an elf," no, of course not, but unknown to himself he put me in the frame of mind to see one, because as everyone knows we're very very close –'

'You are over voluble, and you're making me a little dizzy,' said Miss Mandible. 'Why should an elf obligingly turn up in response to the inner longings of your father?'

'The same way as bacteria turn up and give people colds, I suppose. Not long ago people didn't believe in those, either.'

'This is a fascinating theory, Caterina, but why am I so important to it?'

'Because you are the only person who can understand it.

No, I don't mean understand. You're the only person who can really *feel* it.'

'Am I?' said Miss Mandible. 'Am I indeed. Caterina, don't expound all this to your father, will you?'

'No?'

'No. If this is his deepest secret, let it remain hidden from him. The worst thing you can do to a person is to expose his deepest secret.'

'So much for psychiatry,' remarked Kate.

'Seriously, Caterina.'

'I wasn't going to anyway, but thanks for confirming what I felt about it. What would I do without you?'

'I could say the same of you, *cara mia*,' said Miss Mandible with feeling.


'Right inside your room?' asked Adam.

'On the bookcase.'

'You must have been scared stiff.'

'Yes and no.'

'But it was real? Solid?'

'It was and it wasn't.'

'You'd drive the compilers of questionnaires mad,' said Adam. '"Tick yes or no" – you'd go and tick both.'

'But that's the way it is,' said Kate. 'I mean, take the elf in the picture. It couldn't possibly have really been there, in one colour supplement out of thousands, but it was really there *for me*. OK, back to the all-in-the-mind thing – hallucination? No, because it wasn't *all* in the mind – it wasn't *made* there – it was *put into* the mind by something outside, just as germs are put into your bloodstream. I mean, it was there and it wasn't. I suppose', reflected Kate, 'that that's how religious people have seen visions. They didn't just go dotty and dream them up. They were given them. All to themselves.'

'You'll be a convert yet,' remarked Adam. 'But where are you getting all this from?'

'I think it started when we all met together. I knew that everyone was telling the truth, but everyone had their own angle on the truth, if you see what I mean. And then I remembered what old Mr Hermitage said to us. He said, "Are they real? Don't let them be real." He's been in on all this for a long time, he's got the right idea, but as he said, he's out of his depth. You just can't beat them by will-power. You have to turn a key somewhere.'

'Oh for the key,' said Adam. 'You're amazingly calm, considering, what with the elf actually invading your room and Prof Bodkin bringing up reinforcements –'

'Oh no, he wasn't bringing up reinforcements. He was desperate to break away.'

'From the elf?'

'And from Margot.'

'*What?*'

'I'm sure of it, Adam. He might be the world's greatest authority on fairies but he's not an authority, he's no kind of authority on Margot's nature, and for that matter,' said Kate, 'nor is she.'

'You mean she's been in cahoots with the elves all along?'

'No, no. They don't collaborate, they play with people's weaknesses. I mean it's another case of deep-down-buried wishes. I'm glad Margot used that expression to Aunt Julia. It opened up my mind. I believe her deep-down-buried wish was for Professor Bodkin to fall under a spell.'

'Why?'

'Because she's played second fiddle to him all her life, and she wanted to control him.'

'This is just a hunch,' said Adam.

'I saw it in the Professor's face. He never wanted me as a sacrifice. That was what Margot thought, or rather it was what she thought she thought. She's been deceiving herself and the elves are glad to let her, because they can get two people into their trap instead of one. That poor pathetic old

Professor knows this perfectly well, and he wants me to get him out of it.'

'That tune', said Adam, 'was drumming in my head half the night.'

They stared at each other, thinking the same thought.

'The thing is *when*,' said Adam.

Kate nodded. She felt excited and tantalized, like the desert traveller who sees an oasis that might be a mirage.

Margot watched Jasper's bicycle recede. He wobbled as he went, for he was a sick man and should not be riding it at all. She, too, was sick at heart. Life in the cottage had become like the aftermath of a nuclear disaster, empty and derelict, the awful outcome of a lifetime spent in worship of false gods, for she now believed that she had lived a misunder-standing ever since, at the age of eighteen, she had become the Professor's disciple.

She went back to her duties, fed him with the disgusting liquid food, tended him, and sat before him, staring at him with eyes newly opened. She had hero-worshipped him for more than forty years, and for forty years she had deceived herself.

She had told herself 'trust no one' many times, but it now became 'trust nothing', for, above all, ideas themselves were not to be trusted. She had been wrong about the girl Crimonesi. Margot no longer believed that Kate was to serve as an exchange hostage; she would simply be the elves' second captive. She had been wrong about Jasper, whose death she was bringing about by witchcraft: what harm could he do after all? He of all people was the one she could trust. The word 'kill' echoed in her mind. It had not been meant for the humble Jasper, nor for the Crimonesis. Only one victim remained.

Margot rose, stiffly, and released the brake on the Profes-sor's mobile chair. His one eye rolled in dread, but she got behind him where she could not see it, pushed him to the french windows, opened them, and wheeled him into the garden. She felt sick at what she was doing, together with an evil joy in her power over him. She manoeuvred the chair carefully round the twisting paths until it would go no farther, so that the Professor was in roughly the same place as he had been in the photograph. Then, still avoiding contact with his eye, Margot left him. She wormed her way behind the cupressus trees and stared across the water at the wood.

It happened, whether by accident or the design of fate, that the Crimonesis and Adam were together at this time, in the garden after dinner, enjoying the bland August evening. Or perhaps not entirely enjoying it, for a tumble of thoughts occupied each head while the conversation went on, but they carefully avoided the subject that possessed them all. Guido was asking Adam some questions about music and musicians, Adam was replying earnestly enough, Kate appeared to be listening, and Brenda was taking a private stock of Adam while smiling on him. While they were in this disarmed state the demand of the subject became overwhelming.

Adam stopped in mid-sentence as the image of a mutilated Jasper filled his mind. It was more than mere recollection; the nightmare re-enacted itself, distracting him completely from the waking world. Guido, too, was revisited by a dream: he saw Margot fanged and grinning, and Professor Bodkin like a moving corpse. Kate, who had been spared dreams, was alerted to the trouble in their minds, and Brenda stared at the three of them and trembled.

Kate ran into the house and came back with Adam's flute, which he had brought with him from the tearooms. Thrusting it on him, she cried to her father, 'It's locked! Your bureau. It's locked. Get the picture. Hurry!'

Guido obeyed unquestioningly, and as he ran back with the colour supplement Adam raised his flute to his lips and, at last, began to play.

# CHAPTER FIFTEEN

K ATE HAD SUPPOSED that the elfin tune would be magical, with the concentrated essence of the eerie strains that underlay Adam's rendering of ordinary tunes. In fact it was merely tinkling, like a tedious musical box. Was this *all*?

She had vaguely believed, and so had Adam, that played at the right time, that tune would draw Professor Bodkin out of his bondage. She had visualized the Professor manifesting himself a third time, a liberated ghost, quit of his decrepit and paralysed body and seeing with the eyes of the spirit. If the wraith of him had drifted across their suburban lawn she would hardly have been astonished. But now, staring at Adam, his face puckered over his flute, she felt more excluded from his musical world than ever. He was consumed in his playing. He was not liberating Professor Bodkin, nor her, but only himself.

She huddled on the grass by her deck-chair and gazed at the magazine picture in the fading evening light. Her father crouched beside her. Disillusionment with Adam brought home to her where her deepest allegiance lay. Her heart ached for Guido. Never had she loved him so much.

But the picture was not a talisman to use against the elves. She saw only deceit in it now, as in all their dealings. It was just another item from their store of mischief. The tune was no more of a magic formula than the picture. It

tinkled on, repeating the same phrase. There was, nevertheless, a certain fascination in it. It engendered a helplessness,
a faintness of heart. Kate felt rather panicky, as if she were
sliding gently down a slope and could not stop herself.
When she had fainted in the china shop, she had been
separated from her own body. She must not, she must not
let that happen again, because the force that was drawing
her away here was much stronger. She wanted to cry out to
Adam to stop playing, but she could not, nor was he in any
way in harmony with her. He was exorcising some phantom of his own. She was losing contact with her father, too.
She panted for breath against a feeling of faintness and
fixed her eyes on the picture, for she feared now that if she
looked up she would see the elf again and be unable to resist
it. The tune shifted its stress and adjusted itself to words:
*come away, come away . . .*

She stared at the picture so hard that her eyes became
unfocused and it blurred. She blinked to clear her vision
and saw that something new had come into the scene, to
the left of the Professor, protruding from a hosta. It was not
the elf; it was her own face.

Kate did look up now, and found herself in the garden
with its mound of flowering shrubs and its Albertine rose.
The Professor stood within touching distance of her. With a
strange quirk of reasoning she looked down the garden for
the press photographer who must have been here when the
scene was shot, but what she saw was an indiscriminate
mass, like the background a painter might fill in behind a
portrait. She knew that her parents and Adam were in those
shadows, and that she was cut off from them. She knew
that she was there too, in body, apparently poring over the
picture, but she was here in spirit, and losing herself.

And now the tune became more insistent than ever. It
was no longer being played by Adam. It was unearthly and
overwhelmingly seductive. She turned to the Professor and

found that he was no longer within reach. She had moved several paces nearer to the limit of the garden. She grasped at the words of Jasper: *Don't let them be real, shut them out . . . It sounds hard, but you can do it if you want to.* Jasper's mind was uncluttered and he might well know what was needed, but he certainly couldn't take his own advice; he was as enslaved as everyone else. Nevertheless she clung to his words as her only source of hope. She fought with all the strength of her mind. But she was fighting with the wrong weapon. Reason didn't work.

It is said that in the last stages of drowning the sensation is pleasant. Kate began to have the same experience, feeling the lure of drifting into oblivion. Still she resisted for her father's sake; and as she remembered him, and concentrated on him, a new strength gathered in her, a human strength that the elves lacked.

The tune persisted, but now it was coming from a different direction, as if she had crossed from one loud speaker to another in a stereo system. She heard Adam again, but Adam was only the instrumentalist in this; Adam was in love with her but this was something else and beyond his reach. The theme of *come away* became *come back*, and her father's voice was calling.

And now it was as if the elfin face, in opposition to its usual course, had turned from its aged cynical profile to its simpering frontal look, and had become something not to be taken seriously, a toy for kids. Kate went forward and the mound of shrubs, the figure of the Professor, the whole garden faded and vanished. The flute playing stopped.

Kate straightened up from the photograph and looked at her father. He said quietly, matter-of-factly:

'You came back, then.'

'Yes, I came back,' said Kate, but she knew that she had come back to a new dimension. She had broken a barrier; she was closer to her father than ever before, and free from him too. Brenda looked from one to the other, and, with her sixth sense, understood.

'I've lost the tune,' said Adam.

He was quietly triumphant. 'I've lost it,' he repeated. 'It's gone.'

He cleared his throat. 'I don't know what happened,' he said. 'Something did.'

The three of them looked at him with curious detachment. He felt, somehow, that he must justify himself.

'The dream came back to me,' he said.

Now Kate did give him her full attention. 'Jasper?' she demanded, with a pang.

'No, not Jasper,' said Adam. 'It was the woman screaming.'

Light was failing in the cottage garden and as the sun went down behind the wood, the trees across the water became a darkened mass. Margot stood facing them, motionless and inhuman; she saw pinpoints of light pricking the shadows, thousands of them, winking and glittering. The trees threw long black masses across the lake, but in the lighter strips between them she saw the first entrant, its nose drawing a 'V' behind it as it swam; and then there was a silent invasion of the water, with beady eyes coming nearer and nearer at a steady speed. Margot stayed for a moment to beckon them, her dull black eyes alight.

She worked her way back along the trees to stand by the Professor and found that she was now dreadfully weak, on the brink of collapse. She hung over the crumpled figure of the Professor and saw mortal terror in the one sound eye. She was aghast at what she was doing, but at the same time sick with glee. She looked back and saw between the small gaps in the cupressus trees the glinting of the first battery of eyes.

She turned to the Professor and said softly, 'Adieu.'

But she looked at the eye again.

'Oh no, no,' she whispered.

There was no light in it. It was dead, as dead as the rest of him. She was alone in the garden until the first wave of visitors swept in.

Her screams were so piercing that the owner of the grand house at the other end of Dovecot Lane, who was just returning from a Rotary Club dinner, heard them and telephoned the police.

The police came and Professor Bodkin and Margot were taken to hospital. Although the Professor was beyond caring, frantic efforts were made in the ambulance to save Margot from dying from loss of blood. When she recovered consciousness she was delirious and the doctors forbade anyone to speak to her. They sought out Jasper at 14 Arden Place. The hour, even now, could not be called an unsociable one, but Jasper had taken to going to bed very early and they were some time rousing him. He sat in his living room with an overcoat over his pyjamas and shuddered. He was in shock, they decided. They were used to such cases and ruled out any suggestion that he had been directly responsible.

Nevertheless his answers were odd, as if somehow he had expected this disaster. They told him nothing, in the hope that he might give something away. They were very patient and picked gradually at information.

'She was his secretary, was she, sir?'

'Colleague. But she'd become his nurse.' And Jasper volunteered a few details of the relationship.

'So she'd be quite devoted to him, would you say?'

'She worshipped him.'

'Did she make a practice of wheeling him into the garden of an evening?'

'No, she used to read to him.'

'So that was something exceptional?'

'Don't know why they made her do that.'

'Who do you mean by *they*, sir?'

Jasper replied evasively, 'You can never tell with them.'

It was a shifty sort of answer. But the detective-sergeant, who had heard of Professor Bodkin's book, was beginning to guess at Jasper's state of mind. He had dealt with cases involving the occult before, nasty ones steeped in Black Magic, but he doubted if this was one of those. He let Jasper go back to bed and warned him mildly that he would be back for further questions later.

The following day he and his colleague were allowed to question Margot, very briefly. By now they had organized an extensive search for her attacker but the nature of her injuries made him wonder if any such person existed. For that reason he did not ask the public for information, as is customary, and vouchsafed nothing to the press. From Margot's exhausted mutterings he learned that there was something strange about the wood. He took this quite seriously and had it ransacked for any signs of witchcraft or magical practice. But there were none, nor unusual denizens, only an indigenous rat or two. It was impossible to tell, in the present fine weather, if it really never rained in the wood, but everything seemed normal to the police, who were exchanging quips about the teddy bears' picnic.

By now the doctors were convinced about what had happened to Margot. Jasper, visiting her, asked nervously, 'Was she very badly bitten?'

'*Bitten?*' replied the ward sister. 'She's not been bitten. She mutilated herself with a pair of scissors. She's cut herself half to pieces.'

# CHAPTER SIXTEEN

ALL THE EVIDENCE pointed to this. The wounds had clearly been made by the scissors which Margot had still been clutching in her hand, and they were all in the front of her body and within reach of her striking arm. Had she not been in so weak a condition she would have stabbed herself to death. A frenzied attacker would certainly have done so.

What at first appeared to be the signs of a struggle, the bruised ground and the trampled flowers, had evidently been made by Margot herself as she flung herself about. There were no signs of violence on the Professor. The coroner, without demur, returned a verdict of death from natural causes. What was he – eighty-two, eighty-three? And paralysed for years? His heart had given out. Doubtless the simple act of being wheeled into the garden had been too much for him.

General opinion had it that the shock of the old gentleman's death had unhinged Margot, who had given so many years of her life to him. She now lay calm and sedated in the hospital bed, no longer speaking of fairies or animals with human bodies, indeed hardly speaking at all, but eyeing everybody with profound contempt and offering them no more than monosyllables. She was, of course, given the services of a psychiatrist, whom she treated as an idiot.

The psychiatrist noted that Margot was most at ease with Jasper, who visited her daily. She smiled when he came in.

He could be an aid to her recovery. Unfortunately he encouraged her in her delusion rather than helping her to get rid of it. Indeed he seemed to share it. He was given to cryptic utterances, such as, 'You have to tell yourself they're not real,' which seemed a promising comment, but would then spoil it by adding, 'They know how to get at you, see.' He, too, was obviously affected by his years in the Professor's service.

Jasper's physical condition improved over the visits. He looked to be putting on weight. Something had happened there, thought the psychiatrist. Some imaginary spell had been lifted. It was an interesting case altogether. However, it was best to let sleeping dogs lie, because Jasper's sympathy with Margot was good therapy.

'That woman's a fool,' said Margot of the psychiatrist.

'She's all right,' said Jasper. 'She just doesn't understand.'

'*You* understand, don't you, Jasper?'

'I think so.'

'They told me "Kill",' said Margot. 'They didn't tell me that meant myself.'

'You couldn't help yourself.'

'It's all over, anyway. My lifetime's work.'

'It's for the best.'

'I'm not going back to that cottage.'

'Then you'll have to live somewhere else,' said Jasper placidly.

'I don't want to live alone.'

'No, living alone isn't very nice.'

Kate and her father also visited Margot. They felt no animosity towards her. They even, in this aftermath, felt a certain kinship. And as for kinship, their own was now complete. Kate had often imagined reaching this state of perfect affinity with her father, visualizing it as coming like the drop of a curtain or the fade-out of a film; but in those cases active life ceases, and of course it was nothing like that. To outward appearances, their relationship was much the same, but in essence it was a tranquil state that could not be expressed in words nor measured by mathematics.

Margot, swathed and strapped up, greeted them with a sardonic goodwill that passed for her as cordiality. By good fortune she had not marked her face, and although she looked crumpled and old there was a restfulness about it that had not been there before. One might almost have dared to believe that for the first time in her life Margot was happy.

After some minutes of the halting talk that is common to hospital visits she said abruptly, 'They've gone, you know.'

The Crimonesis nodded.

'Gone,' repeated Margot. 'They've left the wood. Left the planet.'

'I know,' said Kate.

'Yes. You don't believe this pseudo-scientific claptrap about mental states and whatnot?'

'Well . . .' said Kate.

Margot struggled upright and looked at her with a kindling eye. 'You find that difficult to answer,' she said. 'Why is it difficult to answer?'

'Because . . . it's true and it isn't,' said Kate.

'What does that mean?'

Kate hesitated, groping for words, but Margot checked her.

'Don't try to explain. If you really know, there is no explanation.'

'So you *know*, do you?' said Miss Mandible. 'Tell me what you know.'

'A lot of it you've told me already, Auntie,' said Kate. 'They really do exist. You said something about their being a forgotten race with their own culture. That's right, they're real, like the stars that Dad studies, and the life on them, maybe. But they can only get to us through our own minds, and so we make our own versions of them. You knew something like that from the start, better than any of us.'

'It did me no good. They made a fool of me.'

'I think that was because you came near to understanding them, and I guess they hate being understood. Professor Bodkin got round to understanding them, and as Jasper said, look what happened to him. I don't think Margot ever did, not really . . .'

'Why do you say that?'

'I don't know. I don't know enough about it, and I'm never going to find out. I think Margot played along with them for some years, but some time or other she must have broken the rules and they turned on her. Or rather they didn't: they turned her on herself. Don't you see, that was the cruellest thing they could do: they ratted on her, they suddenly pretended they didn't exist and left her to destroy herself. It's their way; they deceive people, they lead them to believe lies, they lead them astray, like the will-o'-the wisp.'

'Yet it seems the Croupe woman is better off for it after all. Why didn't they make her destroy herself completely?'

'Because there was a saving factor that they didn't reckon with.'

'What factor?'

'Love,' said Kate.

'*Love?*' repeated Miss Mandible in a high incredulous tone.

'Conquers all,' said Kate, and laughed at the cliché. 'Who'd have guessed it, eh?'

'Well,' said Miss Mandible rather faintly, 'there aren't so many characters in that scenario that one can't guess who you mean . . . Good Heavens, I wonder if you're right?'

'I've wondered before now why Mr Hermitage stayed around so long,' said Kate. 'He didn't know why either.'

'The strange taste of Mr Hermitage,' remarked Miss Mandible.

'Oh I don't know,' said Kate. 'I think he must have fallen for her caring qualities.'

'I think a moth must feel like I do when it emerges from the chrysalis,' said Adam. 'Reborn. I'm not kidding myself, Katie, I'm playing like an angel, everyone says so. It's been like a fantastic dream. Amazing what the power of the mind can do. Auto-suggestion . . . Your Dad and I must have caught it from you . . . Incredible.'

'So where did I catch it from?' asked Kate.

''E'd be a lucky one as knowed that,' said Adam. (Kate suspected that he was quoting.) 'Womanly fears, I suppose. Don't expect mere males to understand.'

'Adam,' said Kate, 'the mind doesn't just run off its own power. Elves are imagined but not imaginary . . .'

But he was not listening, he was just waiting for her to finish speaking. He had always wished to believe, in the face of all evidence, that the experience had been imaginary and he stuck to it now. 'Well, we're all entitled to our beliefs,' he said. 'All I know is, I'm glad to have got rid of a hang-up.'

This is like falling out of love, thought Kate. You forget all memory of being in it . . .

'I really am playing well, Katie . . .'

'I'm sure you are,' said Kate. He was indeed like the emergent moth, showing his true colours.

He was a good-natured lad with an amusing turn of speech and an attractive gaiety of manner, and he had played a most important part in putting things to rights, but when he had played his mind had not been on her. In fact, when she discounted sexual attraction, which can deceive like nothing else, Kate wondered what there was to him, for he didn't quite come to life. He was in love with a musical instrument.

'I wish you every happiness, the two of you,' she said.

She did not, however, immediately part company with Adam, but left it to time and distance to decide a course. She might yet be mistaken about him. All those involved in the adventure had been in some way mistaken, even the elves. They might be supernatural, but they were not super-human, and there were forces they did not understand. Probably, lacking humanity, they were unable to learn.

As for herself, she was less sure but wiser, a good equation all in all.

She drew her curtains and prepared for bed. She hesi-tated, tempted to open them again and contemplate her five flattering reflections. 'No,' she decided. She didn't want to be flattered.